Long ago he had accepted his life as a loner and dismissed all notions of marriage or raising a family.

For Clint Adams there was no other logical attitude. A man with a reputation like his could never be rid of it. One day the legend of the Gunsmith would surely get him killed . . .

Don't miss any of the lusty, hard-riding action in the Charter Western series, THE GUNSMITH:

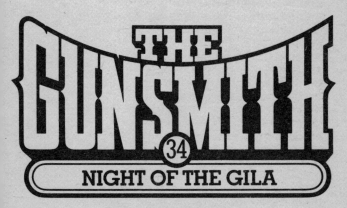

THE GUNSMITH

34

NIGHT OF THE GILA

J.R. ROBERTS

CHARTER BOOKS, NEW YORK

THE GUNSMITH #34: NIGHT OF THE GILA

A Charter Book/published by arrangement with the author

PRINTING HISTORY
Charter Original/November 1984

ISBN: 0-441-30913-5

Charter Books are published by The Berkley Publishing Group,
200 Madison Avenue, New York, N.Y. 10016.
PRINTED IN THE UNITED STATES OF AMERICA

Dedicated to
David Colton

ONE

"I've never been to bed with a genuine living legend before," Cindy Jillian remarked as she unbuttoned her gingham dress.

"I'd rather you just thought of me as a man," the Gunsmith replied, slipping off his denim shirt.

"Kind of have trouble thinking of you as anything else," the woman commented with a smile.

Cindy allowed her eyes to roam over Clint Adams's lean, well-muscled physique. The only sign of his age was in the number of scars which marred his flesh. Tattoos of a hundred violent encounters, the most obvious was a jagged streak on his left cheek.

The Gunsmith had lost count of how many times he had been touched by the icy fingers of Death. One day Clint would be snared within Death's grasp, but he wasn't worried about that. He was too intelligent to believe the hogwash associated with the legend of the Gunsmith, which was no more than a newspaperman's fantasy as far as he was concerned. No man is unbeatable, unkillable or immune to fear.

The legend had started years ago when Clint Adams was a deputy sheriff in Oklahoma. He had already acquired an unwanted reputation as a lightning-fast gunman. Then along came a smart-mouthed newspaperman. Clint had always dabbled in repairing and modifying guns. The newspaper scoop learned about this and labeled Deputy Adams *the Gunsmith*. The writer called this "extra color" for his article.

"Yeah," Clint once remarked to his friend Jim Hickok. "Yellow journalism."

The title plagued Deputy Adams. Law enforcement became too difficult for Clint. Everybody either regarded him as a two-legged mad dog with a gun or they were disappointed if he solved a problem without the use of his own modified double-action pistol. Clint decided to give up his badge and embark on a new career.

He had been a lawman for eighteen years. Clint only had one other trade to fall back on. Ironically, he became a full-time gunsmith. With a wagon which served as a combination home and traveling gunsmith shop, Clint wandered throughout the West and made his living as best he could.

Cindy Jillian was a pioneer wife, like so many others Clint had encountered in his travels. The Gunsmith had met her earlier that day at the Meldorn general store. Her husband had run off two years before and left her to manage the store on her own.

"I don't know where that good-for-nothin' louse

took off to," Cindy had told Clint, "but if he ever shows his face around here again, I'll shoot him dead. That's for sure."

"I believe you," the Gunsmith replied. This was a little white lie. What was the point in telling Cindy that he really guessed she'd take her spouse back in a minute if he returned to Meldorn—something that seemed pretty unlikely to happen. The woman was probably attracted to drifters, men who feared personal commitment and close relationships more than death by slow torture. The Gunsmith certainly fit that category.

For Clint Adams there was no other logical attitude. Long ago he had accepted his life as a loner and dismissed all notions of marriage or raising a family. A man with a reputation like his could never be rid of it. One day the legend of the Gunsmith would surely get him killed.

Cindy had accepted an invitation to have supper with Clint. One of the Gunsmith's skills was the ability to read a woman's attitude. Since he wouldn't be in Meldorn long and never intended to return after he left, Clint decided to speak bluntly and figured she'd agree to another suggestion that evening.

Afterwards he invited her to join him in his hotel room to share a bottle of wine. The young woman responded as he'd hoped she would.

Cindy was in her middle twenties and attractive. She wore her honey-blond hair in a ponytail and her breasts handsomely filled the front of her sky-blue dress. The girl also seemed more than willing to oblige Clint in bed.

If only she would shut up about that living legend crap.

"Folks say you must have killed more men than died at Gettysburg," Cindy commented as she stripped down to her underwear.

"Don't believe everything you hear," Clint replied dryly.

"Is it true you're the fastest gunslinger in the West?" she inquired.

"I don't know," Clint said. "I really don't care too much if there is some fella wandering around who might be faster than me—so long as I don't have to draw against him."

"You knew Wild Bill Hickok, right?" Cindy asked.

"Jim—Wild Bill and I were friends," the Gunsmith confirmed.

Clint gazed over Cindy's shapely naked body. Her breasts were large and firm with rosy nipples. She had a small waist, a rounded belly and full, womanly hips and thighs.

"But you were faster than Hickok?" she inquired.

"I doubt it," Clint replied. "Bill was faster than God."

"What about Wyatt Earp?" Cindy wanted to know as she climbed into the bed.

"I really don't feel like talking about this right now," he confessed. "Mind if we change the subject?"

"Okay." And with that Cindy sat up, shifted about on the bed, and without further ado lowered her face to the Gunsmith's crotch.

No man can ever hope to understand women, the Gunsmith thought as she ran her tongue along his cock which swelled and throbbed inside her mouth. When Clint had had about all he could take he reached down and drew Cindy up over him. He fondled her silky white breasts as she straddled his loins and licked the taut nipples, teasing them gently with teeth and tongue.

Cindy moaned happily and began to grind herself against Clint's pulsating manhood. The Gunsmith's hands slid across her soft smooth skin as he gently stroked the sensitive flesh behind her knees and then her inner thighs.

Clint did not rush lovemaking. He let Cindy decide when she wanted to receive him. At last, she guided him into position and with a moan carefully eased herself onto him. Clint sighed with pleasure as Cindy rocked to and fro, working his cock deeper. She crooned and gasped in pleasure.

The woman increased the tempo of her movements and began to ride him. Then she cried out and raked her fingernails across the mat of hair on Clint's chest. Cindy shuddered violently as an orgasm erupted within her. Clint arched his back and thrust himself into her cavern of delight, twisting his hips as he lunged faster and harder.

Cindy cried out again as a second climax swept through her like summer lightning. Clint finally allowed himself the same luxury and they both moaned in satisfaction.

"Oh, Clint," she whispered as she collapsed across his chest, "that was paradise."

"And we've got all night to make another trip," the Gunsmith replied with a grin.

TWO

Duke whinnied happily when Clint Adams entered the livery stable. The Gunsmith approached Duke's stall and smiled as the magnificent black gelding thrust his head forward. Clint scratched the horse's muzzle.

The Gunsmith had raised the blooded Arabian from a colt and considered Duke to be more than an animal. The horse was Clint's partner.

Clint had paid the hostler to be certain that Duke received the best of care. He found a horse brush and an old blanket and entered the stall to groom Duke.

"Don't get too comfortable, big fella," Clint told his horse as he brushed him. "We're leaving this town after breakfast. You eat more oats while I get some eggs and coffee. Then we'll hit the trail again. How's that sound, fella?"

The horse whinnied with enthusiasm.

"Figured that idea would appeal to you." The Gunsmith grinned as he patted Duke's neck.

"Did I hear you say you're leaving Meldorn, Mr. Adams?" a deep voice with an East Texas drawl inquired.

Clint turned to see two men approach from the entrance of the stable. The pair looked as if they had stepped out of the pages of a dime novel written by a city slicker who had never been west of the Ohio Valley.

Both men were tall with broad shoulders and muscular chests. One fellow also had a pot belly, but he was about twenty years older than his companion. The senior man sported a gray cowhorn-shaped mustache and he wore a corduroy jacket, denim trousers and an ivory-handled six-gun on his hip.

The younger man was clean shaven and clad in a white shirt with a tan vest and Levi pants. He wore a fancy hand-engraved gunbelt with a pistol on each hip. Both men wore white stetsons and had brass badges pinned to their lapels.

"You are Clint Adams?" the elder of the pair inquired. "The Gunsmith?"

"Some folks call me that," Clint admitted. "But I'd just as soon be called by my name."

The Gunsmith stepped from the stall, his right hand dangling near the modified double-action colt on his hip. The younger man stiffened and moved both hands toward his pistols. The older man, however, held up a hand to discourage his partner.

"There's no need to be nervous, Mr. Adams."

"Maybe not," Clint said. "But I paid a visit to the local sheriff when I first came to town. Sort of a custom of mine when I'm in a new place. Figure the law likes to know about strangers in town. I met the sheriff and his deputy. You guys ain't them."

"We're still lawmen," the younger fellow declared.

"Anybody can wear a badge," Clint insisted. "Got any other identification?"

"Captain John Foster," the older man replied as he reached inside his jacket.

"Slowly, Captain," Clint warned, aware the stranger might have a hideout gun under his jacket.

"Texas Rangers," Foster stated, extracting a thin leather folder.

He handed it to Clint. The Gunsmith opened the folder and checked its contents. An identification card confirmed that Foster was indeed an officer in the Texas Rangers. Clint returned it to the captain.

The Gunsmith nodded. "Okay. You guys seem to be genuine. Why are you interested in me?"

"This is Sergeant Linden," Foster introduced his partner. "We've got a problem, Mr. Adams. We think you can help us."

"Well, I'd have to know what kind of help you're talking about," Clint replied.

"What do you know about Gila?" Linden asked in a hard, flat voice which suggested he didn't like talking to the Gunsmith.

"There's a river called the Gila in New Mexico, connected to the Colorado River." Clint shrugged. "Is that what you mean?"

"More like the monster than the river," Linden snorted.

"The gila monster?" Clint raised his eyebrows. "That's a big lizard found throughout the Southwest. Sort of looks like a thick-beaded sausage with legs. Better not keep one for a pet. As far as I know, there are only two types of poisonous lizards in the world. One is the Mexican beaded lizard and the other is the gila monster. Still, I wouldn't leave Texas because old gila hangs out here. Those lizards aren't real common and they don't go hunting for people. Besides, you've got two guns and all the monster has is his fangs. Reckon that ought to make it a fair fight.''

Linden stiffened and glared at Clint.

"Let me explain, Mr. Adams," Foster began quickly. "You see, there is a Mexican bandit who calls himself Gila. Apparently, he was inspired by the reptile with the same name.''

"Name suits him too," Linden added. "That Mex bastard is a cold-blooded killer.''

"And he's leading the most vicious gang of cutthroats ever to cross the border," Foster stated.

"That's a mighty tall claim," the Gunsmith mused. "There have been some real nasty *bandidos* who've slipped over to the States in the past.''

"Like el Espectro?" the captain inquired.

"Yeah," Clint said grimly. "I guess you fellas know about my run-in with "the Ghost." El Espectro was about as bad as a man can be without sprouting horns and a tail." *

"Gila is worse," Foster declared.

"You wouldn't be so sure about that if you'd tangled with el Espectro," the Gunsmith told him.

"Was he bulletproof?" Linden asked with a sneer.

"I don't think so. But there were tall tales that el Espectro was supposed to be Death on horseback. The Grim Reaper with a six-gun and all that superstitious hogwash. He was bad enough without having any supernatural powers.''

*Gunsmith #19: Bandido Blood

"Well, Gila is suppose to be bulletproof, Adams."
Linden smiled. "How's that sound? Afraid to go up
against an opponent you can't take care of with that
fancy double-action pistol of yours?"

"That's enough of that sort of talk, Sergeant,"
Foster snapped. "There's no need to contribute to
those fool stories about Gila."

"What stories?" the Gunsmith inquired.

"Let me explain the *facts* to you first," Foster said.
"Then we can discuss the fairy tales concerning Gila."

"If I have to listen to a long story," Clint remarked,
"I'd rather do it with a beer in my hand. Come on. I'll
let you fellas buy me a drink."

The two Rangers followed Clint Adams to the local
saloon. Sergeant Linden was clearly irritated by Clint's
behavior, but the senior Ranger took it all in stride.
Foster bought a pitcher of beer and all three men moved
to a table.

The Gunsmith hadn't really been anxious for a
drink. He had suggested the saloon simply because he
wanted to see if the Rangers would agree to his request.
That they had suggested they were under orders to
oblige Clint, and try to gain his help.

The Texas Rangers did not have a reputation for
asking civilians for help. They hardly needed to. The
Rangers were a tough, well-trained corps of profes-
sionals. Gila must be quite a *bandido* indeed if the
Texas Rangers couldn't handle him.

Clint also moved the discussion to the saloon because it put the Rangers in an environment which
reduced their sense of authority. As Clint thought they
might, Foster and Linden had removed their badges

before they entered the tavern to avoid attracting attention. Besides, it's bad for a lawman to be seen drinking while on duty. But no Ranger is comfortable without his brass star pinned to his chest.

The Rangers were used to taking and giving orders in a paramilitary manner. They were not accustomed to doing business in a civilian atmosphere. The Gunsmith, however, was right at home in the saloon. The Rangers obviously felt awkward here, but, Clint thought with a smile, he himself was as comfortable as a pig in shit.

"Okay," the Gunsmith began. "Tell me about Gila."

"Not much to tell," Foster said. "Nobody ever heard of the bastard until about a month ago. That's when Gila and his band launched their first raid. They hit a small Texas cattle ranch near the border which belonged to a fellow named Alan Dobbs."

"Were they after the cattle?" Clint inquired.

"If they was just a bunch of cow thieves we wouldn't be askin' you for help, Adams," Linden said curtly. "Cattle rustlers ain't much of a problem for the Texas Rangers."

"Gila and his men don't seem to have much interest in livestock," Foster explained. "They came to kill. The bandits gunned down some cowboys who were working the herd in the grazing land. They were the lucky ones. They died quickly. Then the gang headed straight for the ranch house. That's where the blood-bath really occurred."

"The women were raped and murdered," Linden continued. "Several men were tortured. Skinned alive. Then the bandits worked 'em over with red-hot branding irons. Mighty mean bunch of sons of bitches in Gila's crew.''

"If the bandits killed everybody," Clint began, "how do you know this Gila character did it?"

"There were three small children in the Dobbs family," Foster said grimly. "Gila spared them."

"And the kids saw it all?" the Gunsmith asked.

"Yes." Foster nodded.

"Then he didn't spare them very much," Clint said.

"The bandits also planted a banner," the Ranger captain explained. "A crude flag with a stout lizard drawn on white cloth. It was the sketch of a gila monster with a blunt snout and a thick tail."

"The massacre at the Dobbs spread was just the beginning," Linden declared. "Three more ranches have been hit since. The last one happened just two days ago. The Webber spread ain't more than ten miles from here. Gila slaughtered everybody there, 'cept the kids.''

"We don't know why the bandits don't kill the children." Foster shrugged. "Maybe it's Gila's idea of showing mercy."

"*Machismo*," Clint told him. "Mexican *bandidos* have a funny idea about what's manly. *Bandidos* think killing a man is *macho*. They don't seem to figure it makes much difference whether it's self-defense or outright murder. It's real *macho* to have sex with as many women as possible too."

"And the bandits don't see anything wrong with rape either?" Linden inquired.

"*Bandidos* might enjoy rape better than sex with a willing partner," the Gunsmith answered. "They're certainly violent by nature or they wouldn't be bandits in the first place. Could be they find it more exciting if a woman puts up a struggle.''

Linden sneered. ''You sure seem to understand greaser bandits.''

''Mexican hootowls aren't any different from any other brand of asshole,'' Clint stated. ''I've tangled with enough variety to know that. Small-time gunhawks or Corsican gangsters . . . they're all the same type of trash.''

''You didn't explain what the bandits' odd ideas about *machismo* have to do with leaving the children alive,'' Foster reminded him.

''Children aren't worth killing. They're little fish that are thrown back into the lake so they can grow big enough to eat some other time. Besides, kids have vivid memories and over the years their minds will exaggerate all the gory details. They'll tell the grisly tales of the *bandidos*' deeds over and over again. This helps to add to the gang's reputation.''

''So the bastards consider that a sort of fame?'' Foster inquired.

''Something like that,'' the Gunsmith confirmed. ''It also contributes to the general fear folks have toward a particular gang. *Bandidos* want folks to be terrified of them, especially those gangs that prey on *peónes*. They want the peasants to be too frightened to go to the *federales* or the *rurales* for help.''

''Gila certainly isn't following that pattern,'' Foster remarked.

''And there must be a reason for that,'' the Gunsmith stated.

''They're just a bunch of mad dogs,'' Linden snorted. ''Simple as that.''

"A lone mad man might kill people without any motive . . . or at least none that makes any sense to a sane man," Clint replied. "But a whole gang would have to have a reason to follow him. The bandits are following a pattern and they're taking a hell of a risk in order to launch raids on American soil."

"We believe the bandits have robbed the homes of the ranches they've raided," Foster said. "They've always destroyed so much property it's difficult to say what they took before setting a house on fire."

"Well," the Gunsmith mused, "the bandits may have figured they'd find plenty worth stealing in the houses. Maybe they did. Money, silverware, gold coins, whatever. Sure be easier to haul that kind of stuff across the border than herding cattle back to Mexico."

"That's what we figure too," Linden commented. "You're not telling us anything we didn't already know."

"Then tell me something *I* don't know," Clint replied. "Like what the hell do you guys want me to do?"

"Gila has managed to slip past us time and time again," Foster stated. "The border is too big to patrol effectively. Even the Texas Rangers can't be everywhere at once."

"Oh, shit," the Gunsmith groaned. "You want me to go to Mexico and hunt the bastard down, right?"

"Well," Foster began awkwardly, "you handled a similar job for Andrew Woodland a couple of years ago. He paid you two and a half thousand dollars to rescue his daughter from el Espectro."

"The Rangers will pay you four thousand, Adams,"

Linden added, a trace of resentment in his voice.

"I didn't go up against el Espectro for the money,"
Clint told them.

"But you didn't refuse it either," the sergeant
sneered.

In fact, the Gunsmith had given a thousand dollars of
his reward money to the widow of Juan Lopez, a poor
Mexican who had acted as Clint's translator and guide
when he'd gone after el Espectro. The Gunsmith didn't
bother to explain this to Linden. The surly Ranger
would not have believed him.

"Thanks for the drink, Captain," Clint said. "But I
think you fellas have the wrong idea about how I make
my living. I'm not a gun for hire."

"We meant no offense, Mr. Adams," Foster assured him.

"Maybe *you* didn't," the Gunsmith said. "I don't
figure the same is true about the sergeant here."

"Christ," Linden snorted. "I didn't reckon you'd
be so sensitive, Adams."

"I just don't care for rude behavior, fella," Clint
told him. "But I'm hardly the best choice for a mission
into Mexico anyway. Hell, I only speak a handful of
words in Spanish and I'm not really familiar with the
country."

"You're familiar with el Barriga del Diablo," Foster stated.

"The Devil's Belly." Clint rolled his eyes toward
the ceiling. "That's the desert region where el Espectro's headquarters was located."

"You remember it?" the captain inquired.

"Anybody who has ever been in that hellhole re-
members it," the Gunsmith confirmed. "You have

nightmares about that place for the rest of your life. It's the most formidable, inhospitable chunk of sand and rock in the whole goddamn world. The sun can boil you alive and there are rattlesnakes and scorpions crawling all over the place. The Yaqui Indians in the Devil's Belly make our Mescalero Apaches look like old ladies.''

"Before you decide," Foster urged, "I want to assure you that four other men will accompany you into Mexico. They're all good with a gun. Three of them also speak Spanish fluently.''

"Are they Texas Rangers?" Clint inquired.

"Of course not," Foster replied. "Mexico is out of our jurisdiction. Neither the Rangers nor the United States cavalry can legally cross the border. We would have done so already and taken care of Gila by now if we didn't have to work under that restriction.''

"So you want us to do the job instead." The Gunsmith shook his head. "Figure it's okay if we butt heads with the *federales* because it won't reflect on the Rangers? You know how the military operates down there. Piss off a *federale* and you're facing a firing squad the next morning . . . unless he decides just to shoot you right then and there.''

Linden shrugged. "So don't upset any Mex soldiers.''

"A lot of *federales* hate your guts just because you're a *gringo*," Clint answered. "And they don't like Anglos coming into their country to butt into their authority. I doubt that you fellas would like it if *federales* came up north to poke their noses around your turf either.''

"But you're on friendly terms with President Juarez

and General Moreno in Mexico City," Foster declared. "That's another reason we've come to you for help. You're in good graces with the Mexican authorities because you returned that stolen gold shipment to their national treasury." *

"How far do you think that's going to influence the authorities?" Clint inquired.

"General Moreno has already agreed to supply what assistance he can," Foster replied simply. "We received a telegram from Mexico City confirming this just yesterday."

"I'd have to be crazy to go back to el Barriga del Diablo," the Gunsmith muttered.

"You're the only man who can stop Gila, Mr. Adams," Foster said.

Clint grunted sourly and swallowed the last of his beer. He stared down at the empty mug for almost a minute before he spoke.

"These bandits are murdering innocent people and leaving kids orphaned." Clint sighed. "If there's any chance I can stop that from continuing, I suppose I'd feel pretty bad if I didn't try."

"Thank you, Mr. Adams," the captain said sincerely.

"Thank me when it's over," the Gunsmith said bluntly. "*If* I'm still around to thank."

*Gunsmith #15: Bandit Gold

THREE

The Rangers took Clint Adams to meet the men who would accompany him into Mexico. They were waiting for Clint at a corral behind the livery. The Gunsmith could have been happier with the selection of companions.

He recognized one of them right off. He had seen the man's hatchet face once before, in El Paso. His icy blue eyes peered out from hooded lids and a drooping black mustache decorated a hard mouth which resembled a knife wound. It was not the sort of face one forgets—no matter how hard one tries.

"Manuel Sharp?" the Gunsmith asked.

"Wondered if you'd remember me," the killer replied. A cold smile appeared on his ax-blade face. "You were in El Paso when I hauled in Jonah King. Got seven hundred dollars for that hootowl."

"As I recall the sheriff wasn't too thrilled about paying the bounty on that one," Clint mused. "You shot King in the leg and then slit his throat with a straight razor.''

Sharp shrugged. ''Wanted posters say 'dead or alive'. Don't make no difference to me. Hey, Adams. You ever heard of Benjamin Stahl?''

''Thought this might be him,'' Clint remarked as he turned to face the short, wiry figure who stood beside Sharp.

Stahl was a sour-faced Virginian who carried an old Remington revolving rifle. Clint had heard that Stahl had taken the tarnished old percussion weapon from his father's corpse after Yankees had destroyed the old man's house. Stahl had carried that rifle throughout the War Between the States. He earned a reputation as an expert sniper and still made his living with the Remington longarm. Apparently he relied on his rifle marksmanship because he didn't carry a six-gun.

''Heard you and Sharp worked together,'' the Gunsmith remarked.

''Once in a while,'' Stahl said simply. ''We're both loners, but we happened to be in the same area when the Rangers started looking for recruits to take care of this Gila bastard.''

''Lucky I was around,'' Sharp snorted. ''Stahl don't speak Spanish, but I was raised to speak my mama's language as good as my pa's.''

''I speak Spanish too, Sharp,'' a hawk-faced man with shoulder-length black hair and pale green eyes announced. ''And about half a dozen Indian tongues.''

''Sure, Moonlance,'' Sharp snorted. ''But Yaqui ain't one of 'em.''

Clint had heard of Joe Moonlance as well. Half white and half Comanche, Moonlance was a successful bounty hunter who favored a Winchester for long-range kills and a tomahawk for close quarters. Some said Moonlance had inherited the stealth and cunning of the Comanche combined with the ruthlessness and greed of the white man.

The Gunsmith figured Moonlance was just a mean son of a bitch. He was certain this description fit Sharp and Stahl. However, Gila and his gang were far worse than the bounty hunters, and you don't take on a gang of vicious *bandidos* with a bunch of choirboys.

"Guess I'm the only feller here who ain't famous," the fourth man commented. "Name's Stark Collins, Mr. Adams."

Collins was the youngest of the group. His round face seemed like a soft base for two hazel eyes divided by a narrow nose. Collins's straw-colored hair and wide grin contributed to an innocent appearance. Yeah, the Gunsmith thought. A rattlesnake looks like an innocent lump of rock until you see its fangs.

"What are you, Collins?" the Gunsmith inquired. "Gunfighter or bounty hunter?"

The youth smiled. "Maybe I'm both. Reckon I'll figure that out after this is over. Don't really make much difference on this job, does it?"

"Yeah," Clint said. "But you'd do better if you didn't choose either one for a career."

"Hell, you've done okay, Mr. Adams," Collins said.

"I could have done better without having a reputation I never wanted," the Gunsmith told him.

"Who cares about a rep?" Sharp said bluntly. "So long as I get paid, I don't give a shit."

"Who's gonna be head ramrod when we cross into

Mexico?'' Stahl asked the Rangers.

"Adams is in charge all the way," Captain Foster replied.

"He doesn't even speak Spanish," Moonlance complained. "And I bet me and Sharp know Mexico better than he does. Why should Adams be in charge?"

"Because that's what we want," Foster said simply. "And we're paying you to do a job. So you'll do it the way we tell you. Understand?"

"Never argue with the man payin' the wages," Sharp said as he began to roll himself a cigarette. "So when do we head for Mexico?"

"As soon as Adams is ready," Foster said.

"Before we leave," Clint began, "I want to know everything you can tell me about Gila."

"We've told you everything we know," the captain insisted. "Apparently Gila has about twenty men in his gang but we have no solid details about any of them. Hoofprints suggest most of the horses are mustangs, a favorite among *bandidos*. Their weapons vary—rifles, shotguns, pistols, machetes and knives."

"And we know those greaser bastards enjoy torturing people," Linden added.

Sharp's right hand suddenly flashed to the Colt Dragoon on his hip. He drew the weapon in a single fast, smooth motion and cocked the hammer as he aimed the pistol at Linden's face.

"Maybe you didn't hear me say my ma was Mexican, feller," Sharp hissed.

"Jesus," Linden gasped, startled by the bounty hunter's deadly speed and ruthlessness.

"We're discussing business, Sharp," Clint sighed. "Either shoot the sergeant or put the gun away."

"I don't want to hear any more remarks about Mexicans," Sharp growled, but he returned his Dragoon to its holster.

"Did the children who survived the raids give a consistent description of any of the bandits?" the Gunsmith asked. "Especially Gila?"

"They all said Gila was very ugly," Foster replied. "Apparently his nose has been broken and bent out of shape and his face is scarred. They claim he wears a breastplate of some sort, like an iron barrel around his chest and belly."

"Armor?" Clint raised his eyebrows. "Are you serious? This bandit chief is running around wearing a suit of armor?"

"You think that's funny, Adams?" Linden inquired. "Two of those kids say they saw a feller shoot Gila point-blank in the chest. The bandit didn't even grunt."

"Bullshit," Stahl muttered. "Those tin plates won't stop a bullet, for crissake."

"Gila isn't exactly wearing a suit of armor," Foster explained. "It sounds like a type of breastplate."

"Maybe one of those outfits the *conquistadores* used to wear when they whupped the Aztecs," Sharp mused. "The armor is made of copper or something like that. Stahl's right though—never stop a bullet. Those kids must have exaggerated. Guy probably took a shot at Gila and missed. The *bandido* is just wearing that armor for showmanship."

"His gauntlets aren't an exaggeration," Linden declared.

"Gauntlets?" Clint asked.

"Gloves made of chain mail," Foster explained.

"The children claimed the gauntlets extend to the elbow and they're studded with steel spikes."

"More bullshit," Sharp snorted as he spat out a bit of tobacco.

"My ass," Linden snapped. "Some of the victims of the bandit raids were ripped to shreds. They looked like they'd been mauled by a gang of mountain lions."

"So we won't try to arm wrestle with the son of a bitch," Stahl said as he stroked the barrel of his Remington rifle.

"Yeah." Sharp nodded, patting the Colt Dragoon on his hip. "We'll just shoot the bastard on sight."

"Have to find him first," Stark Collins commented.

"Finding Gila won't be hard," Moonlance replied. "A man with an iron chest and spikes on his wrists will be easy to find."

"I believe you gentlemen are ready to go," Foster remarked. "You all understand the mission?"

"Not really complicated," the Gunsmith said. "We're supposed to bring back Gila—dead or alive."

"Ain't gonna bring a mad dog like that jasper back alive," Sharp stated. "We'll have to kill him for sure."

"Yeah," Clint was forced to agree. "If he doesn't kill us first."

FOUR

The Gunsmith and his four man "posse" crossed the border into Mexico later that afternoon. Clint didn't like the way Joe Moonlance gazed at Duke. The half-breed had bragged about his prize Appaloosa stallion until he saw the Gunsmith's gelding. The Appaloosa was indeed a fine horse, but it looked like a broken-down nag compared to Duke.

"When we get back," Moonlance said, "I'll pay you a thousand dollars for the black horse."

"Duke isn't for sale," Clint replied.

"You can buy twenty horses with a thousand dollars," the half-breed told him.

"*You* buy twenty horses. I'll keep Duke."

Moonlance shrugged. Clint realized that the bounty hunter wouldn't simply forget about Duke. After they took care of Gila, Clint would have to watch out for the others in his group. Moonlance wouldn't have any qualms about killing him to get his hands on Duke. The

Gunsmith was equally suspicious of Sharp and Stahl, both of whom were totally ruthless. Greed would always be their main motivation in life. The pair were not truly friends, but they had developed a sense of unity which meant they'd stick together as long as it seemed profitable to both. If the pair figured they could collect a larger share of the reward by eliminating the other three, Sharp and Stahl would not hesitate to do so.

Stark Collins was the only unknown factor, but Clint didn't find any comfort in that. He couldn't trust the kid. However, the Gunsmith didn't worry about any of them trying to shoot him in the back—yet. They would all want the Gunsmith alive until they'd completed their mission.

The five men rode toward Grajo, a small town in the Mexican state of Sonora. Clint glanced about at the sand, rocks and sagebrush. There was nothing unusual about the prairie, yet the Gunsmith felt an uneasy sense of déjà vu.

He had made this journey once before, to rescue Marsha Woodland from el Espectro. That job had been pure hell. Vicious battles, torture and treachery had made it one of the most grueling and dangerous tasks Clint had ever undertaken.

The present mission seemed a bit easier. El Espectro had been an evil genius with fifty men under his command and connections among the regional *rurales*. Gila's gang was reported to be less than half the size of the Ghost's outfit. Although Gila might be just as ruthless and even more brutal than el Espectro, it was doubtful that he was as intelligent as the brilliant albino *bandido*. It was also unlikely that a brute like Gila would have solid connections with the *rurales* or the *federales*.

But Clint knew he couldn't assume Gila would be a pushover. Nothing is easy that takes place in the murderous desert known as the Devil's Belly.

Twilight tinted the sky as the five men approached Grajo. The town was a collection of small adobe buildings. A pair of young children shooed a number of chickens off the street. They herded the birds to a chicken coop located behind one of the huts.

Several *peónes* peered out from doorways to stare at the approaching strangers. The peasants cowered in the shadows. One man doffed his sombrero and hastily crossed himself.

"Don't see any *rurales* around," Sharp commented with a cruel grin. "Reckon these *peónes* are shit-scared of us."

"They don't have any reason to be," Clint stated. "We didn't come here to cause them any harm."

"They don't know that," Stahl remarked with amusement as he slid his Remington revolving rifle from its scabbard.

"Put that thing away," Clint told him.

"The hell I will," Stahl snapped. "There might be bandits hiding in those buildings."

"Bullshit," Clint growled. "These are just *peónes*. Three of you guys speak Spanish. Tell these people why we are here."

"They're *peónes*." Moonlance shrugged. "They're scared of everybody and everything."

"I'm in charge, remember?" the Gunsmith insisted. "Now, tell them we're here in peace."

"Okay, Clint," Stark Collins agreed.

The young gunman called out to the *peónes* in Spanish. Clint understood little of what he said, but he didn't catch any threatening words. After Collins completed his speech, two *peónes* timidly stepped forward.

"Welcome to Grajo," the senior of the pair greeted in broken English. "How may we help you?"

"We're looking for *bandidos, señor*," the Gunsmith replied. "A very evil man who calls himself Gila. He leads a gang of bad *hombres*. We want to stop these men before they hurt more innocent people."

"*Sí, señor*," the old man nodded. "We have heard of Gila, but this *bandido* has never come to Grajo. We can thank God and the Holy Virgin for that."

"Do you have any idea where we might find Gila?" Sharp asked.

"The *bandidos* are in el Barriga del Diablo," the village elder answered. "The desert of the Devil has spawned such evil before."

"I know," Clint stated. "I helped to send el Espectro back to Hell."

"Then you are the Gunsmith?" The old man's eyes widened.

"That's what some folks call me," Clint admitted.

"We have heard of you, *señor*," the elder declared. "It is an honor to have you here in Grajo."

"Then you should be happy to hear we're gonna honor this village by spending the night here," Sharp declared as he swung down from the back of his roan Morgan.

"We don't need to stay here," Clint Adams stated.

"We will be happy to have you spend the night," the old man urged.

"I sure hope you don't have reason to regret that decision, fella," the Gunsmith muttered under his breath.

FIVE

"Mr. Adams?" Stark Collins began as he sat at a table next to Clint. "The old man seems to figure you're a real hero because of that business with el Espectro."

"Things get exaggerated when stories are told too often," the Gunsmith replied, sipping beer from a clay mug.

Clint and the four bounty hunters were in the town's small cantina where the villagers were supplying them with free food and drink. The Gunsmith shared a table with Collins and Joe Moonlance. He kept his back to the wall and drank sparingly. Moonlance filled the bowl of a briar pipe with the pungent herb the Mexicans called marijuana. He puffed on it docilely as young Collins unsuccessfully tried to strike up a conversation.

Sharp and Stahl sat at another table. The ax-faced killer leered at the pretty teenage girl who served them *carne de carnero* and *tortillas,* and *cerveza* to drink with the meal. Stahl seemed to ignore the girl as he polished the frame of his rifle.

The Gunsmith didn't like the way Sharp eyed the waitress, although he couldn't blame the bounty hunter for having carnal thoughts about the girl. She admirably filled a drab peasant dress. Her breasts were large and round. The girl's hips were wide and her figure had a pleasant hourglass shape.

However, Clint didn't consider the circumstances to be proper for romancing a young lady. He was not the sort to force himself on a woman, but he wasn't so certain about the others . . . especially Manuel Sharp.

"*Señorita,*" Sharp called to the girl, gesturing for her to approach.

"*Sí, señor,*" the waitress replied as she drew closer.

"*Quién es?*" he inquired.

"I am Lupe, *señor,*" she replied nervously.

"Ask her how much it'll cost," Stahl told his companion.

"We're honored guests, remember?" Sharp smiled. "Ain't gonna cost us nothin'."

"What do you mean, *señor*?" Lupe inquired.

"You ain't figured it out yet?" Sharp snorted. "Hope you're better in bed than you are at trying to think, you dumb bitch."

"Leave the girl alone," Clint ordered as he rose from his chair.

"Mind your own business, Adams," Sharp growled.

The bounty hunter's left hand snaked out and grabbed Lupe's breast. The girl gasped and tried to pull away. Sharp dug his fingers into the soft mound.

Lupe's features contorted in pain.

"That's enough, Sharp," Clint snapped as he moved toward the bounty killer.

"*Por favor, señor,*" Lupe begged, tears trickling down her cheeks.

"Hell." Sharp grinned. "She's eager for it."

"Let go of the girl or reach for you gun, Sharp," Clint warned.

His hand fell to the modified double-action Colt on his hip. Sharp glared at Clint. His cold blue eyes narrowed. The killer smiled without mirth. Sharp shoved Lupe. She staggered backward into a wall.

"Happy, Adams?" Sharp asked smugly.

His right hand slithered under the table.

The Gunsmith saw Sharp's shoulder jerk backward as the bounty hunter pulled his Dragoon from leather. Clint's gun appeared in his fist so fast no one even saw a blur of movement. The modified Colt roared. Wood splintered from the table top in front of Sharp.

"Oh, shit!" the bounty man screamed as he toppled from his chair.

Sharp's revolver skidded across the floor. His left hand clutched his right forearm. Blood dripped from the bullet-torn flesh and a splinter of broken bone jutted from the ripped sleeve.

Stahl suddenly raised his Remington revolving rifle and swung the old percussion gun toward the Gunsmith. Clint hadn't ignored the Virginia-bred killer. He saw the new threat via the corner of an eye and whirled to face Stahl.

The Gunsmith's pistol snarled once again. A .45-caliber slug slammed into the frame of the Remington rifle. The cylinder exploded from the iron framework.

Stahl dropped the wrecked rifle. His mouth fell open in astonishment.

"My pa's gun!" he shrieked. "You busted Pa's gun!" Sharp bellowed in bestial rage. The bounty killer charged at Clint, a straight razor in his left fist.

"You gotta be kidding," the Gunsmith hissed.

He shot Sharp through the heart. The razor slipped from the bounty hunter's fingers as he stumbled backward into a table. Manuel Sharp placed his hand to the bullet wound in his chest.

"I'll be damned," he whispered as he slumped to the floor and died.

"Wouldn't surprise me if you are," Clint muttered.

"You bastard!" Stahl screamed.

The Virginian didn't carry a pistol or even a sheath knife, yet he was overwhelmed with anger. He had pulled his bandanna from his neck and held the neckerchief in his fists. Stahl twisted the cloth into a thick cord as he lunged for the Gunsmith.

Clint thrust his left forearm into the neckerchief. Stahl's bandanna snared the Gunsmith's wrist. Before the bounty hunter could react to Clint's move, the Gunsmith slapped the barrel of his Colt across the side of his opponent's head. The gunman groaned and fell to the floor unconscious.

"Sweet Jesus," Stark Collins gasped. "I didn't figure anybody could take Sharp and Stahl at the same time."

The Gunsmith didn't reply. He felt no satisfaction in the victory over the two bounty hunters. They had barely started their search for Gila and they had already begun to kill each other.

SIX

"Ain't right to steal from a dead man," Stark Collins declared as he watched Joe Moonlance dump out the contents of two saddlebags.

"Sharp don't need none of this stuff now," Moonlance replied gruffly. "And he'd help himself to any of our belongings if we'd been killed instead."

"Ain't right," Collins repeated. He turned to the Gunsmith. "You going to let him do this, Mr. Adams?"

Clint glanced down at Sharp's belongings on the floor: wanted posters, a box of .44 cartridges, some beef jerky, tin cans of tomatoes and sardines. However, Clint was only interested in a set of handcuffs and leg irons.

"I don't figure it's worth arguing about," the Gunsmith stated as he gathered up the manacles. "Moonlance can have whatever he wants except these irons."

"What are you going to do with them?" Collins frowned.

Clint knelt beside the unconscious figure of Ben Stahl. The Gunsmith cuffed the bounty hunter's wrists together at the small of his back. He frisked Stahl, but found no hideout weapons.

"We going to spend the night here or do you figure we oughta move on?" Collins asked.

"After causing such a ruckus?" the Gunsmith shook his head. "I'd say we've worn out our welcome in Grajo. Let's go."

"What about Sharp?" Collins glanced down at the slain bounty hunter. "We gonna take him back to Texas to be buried?"

Clint sighed and shook his head again. The kid sure as hell didn't sound like a bounty hunter. Collins was either very young, or his innocence was a charade.

"We'll bury Sharp here," Clint declared. "Reckon we'd better turn Stahl over to the *federales*. Maybe they'll take him back across the border for us."

"Maybe." Moonlance shrugged. "I ain't gonna help you bury Sharp, Adams. You killed him. You bury him."

"That's a fact," the Gunsmith agreed.

Clint patted down the long mound of dirt with a shovel. The Gunsmith gazed down at the grave which contained Manuel Sharp. He removed his stetson and held it to his chest solemnly for a moment, in silence.

The Gunsmith left the gravesite and headed for a toolshed. He put the shovel away and prepared to close the door. A faint rustle of cloth alerted Clint that someone lurked behind him.

He reacted instantly. The Gunsmith dropped into a crouch. Simultaneously, he pivoted and drew his Colt in a single, swift, fluid motion.

"Madre de Dios!" Lupe gasped, staring into the muzzle of Clint's pistol. "I am not armed, *señor*."

"Oh," the Gunsmith muttered lamely. He returned his revolver to leather. "You just startled me, ma'am."

"I wanted to thank you for coming to my rescue," the girl explained with a shy smile.

"Sure," Clint replied. He gazed down at her lovely face. "That is, you're welcome. I was glad to help."

"You are very brave, *señor*," Lupe told him as she drew closer.

The girl suddenly wrapped her arms around the Gunsmith's neck. Her lips pressed against his. Clint was surprised by her boldness. Lupe thrust her tongue deep into his mouth. The Gunsmith automatically returned the gesture with equal enthusiasm.

Lupe's fingers slipped between Clint's thighs. He felt her touch his manhood. She stroked it until his member hardened. The Gunsmith rubbed a hand along her torso to her breasts. He gently massaged the ripe mounds. Lupe's nipples felt like brass studs between his fingertips. The girl began to unbutton his trousers.

They broke the embrace gently. The girl slowly slid down his body to kneel before the Gunsmith. She freed his swollen penis and Clint trembled as Lupe closed her lips around him.

Lupe sucked him tenderly. The Gunsmith gasped as Lupe's head moved faster. She pumped his cock with steady, smooth strokes until the Gunsmith's seed exploded inside Lupe's mouth. She drank him without complaint and milked Clint's penis until he felt drained of semen.

"Thank you again, *señor*," she said softly as she climbed to her feet.

"You didn't have to do anything like that," he told her, putting his limp member inside his pants.

"You enjoyed it, *señor*?" Lupe inquired.

"Call me Clint," he replied. "And of course I enjoyed it."

"I did too, Clint." The girl smiled. "You do not think I am a *puta*? A slut, no?"

"No," he assured her. "I think you're lovely and passionate."

"You are lovely too," the girl stated, patting his crotch. "But I am glad you will leave in the morning. It would be awkward for me if you stayed."

"We planned to ride on tonight," Clint explained.

"There is no need for that," Lupe said. "We are not angry and we do not blame you for what happened in the cantina. You killed the evil man, Clint. You and your friends are welcome to stay until morning."

"That's mighty generous of you folks," the Gunsmith said. "We're obliged to you all."

"And I am grateful to you, Clint," Lupe assured him.

She kissed him quickly on the lips. Then she turned and hurried back to the cantina.

Clint never saw her again.

SEVEN

Ben Stahl's eyes blazed hatred when he glared up at the Gunsmith. The bounty hunter was held to the wooden post of a corral by the leg irons and wrist manacles.

"Unchain me, Adams," he challenged. "Give me a fighting chance if you're man enough."

"I was man enough to kick your ass and chain you up," Clint replied simply as he tightened the cinch to Duke's saddle. "So I don't figure I have to do it again."

"You two plan on riding with this bastard?" Stahl asked Joe Moonlance and Stark Collins.

The half-breed glanced up at the morning sky. He shrugged and adjusted the tomahawk in his belt. Then he climbed onto the back of his Appaloosa.

"Daybreak was an hour ago," Moonlance remarked. "Time to move on. We have a job to do, Stahl."

"Joe's right," Collins agreed, mounting his horse. "Sorry, Ben. Looks like you dealt yourself a losing hand that put you out of this bounty hunt."

"You're just gonna leave me shackled to this fence?" Stahl demanded.

"The villagers will turn you over to the *federales*," Clint told him. "When they tell the soldiers that Clint Adams is a friend of General Moreno in Mexico City, the *federales* will listen up. I'm requesting that you be transported back to the border and expelled from the country."

"And you really think they'll do it, Adams?" Stahl asked sourly.

"I'm sure they will. Unless they decide to haul your ass to Fort Morales to throw you into a cell until they can decide what to do with you. You'll be lucky if they remember to feed a gringo prisoner who doesn't speak Spanish. Better be a good boy, Stahl."

"You son of a bitch," the bounty hunter hissed. "You'd better hope Gila and his boys kill you. If they don't, I'll track you down and make you wish your ma and pa had never met each other, Adams."

"You won't be tracking down anybody for a while, Stahl," Clint said as he climbed onto Duke. "Reckon I'll just have to worry about you in the future."

The Gunsmith, Collins and Moonlance rode from the village. Stahl struggled against the bonds which held him to the post. He stood as erect as possible and watched the trio depart.

"You ain't seen the last of me, Adams!" Stahl shouted.

"I have for now," Clint called over his shoulder.

●   ●   ●

The noon sun bathed the trio with merciless heat as they rode into the pitiless inferno known as el Barriga del Diablo. The Gunsmith dismounted. He carried two canteens strapped to the horn of his saddle. Clint opened one and poured some water into his hat. He offered it to Duke. The horse eagerly drank.

"This is the Devil's Belly," Clint told his companions. "From here on, you'd better be on your toes. Everything in this place is dangerous."

"I've been in deserts before, Adams," Moonlance grunted.

"Not in this one," the Gunsmith stated. "Assume every rock might have a Yaqùi hiding behind it. They're all over the desert. Might be watching us right now."

"Figure they'll attack?" Collins asked.

"Maybe," Clint replied. "If we're lucky, they'll just let us ride through. Hard to say for sure. Reckon it depends on whether they want anything we've got. Horses, guns, water, supplies. Might just decide to kill us for the hell of it."

"Don't see much call to worry about a bunch of half-naked savages," Collins remarked.

"You wouldn't feel that way if you'd ever seen what Yaqui do to their victims," the Gunsmith warned. "First time I was in el Barriga del Diablo I saw a couple of victims of Yaqui torture. The Indians had cut off one fella's head and stuck it on the end of a pole. Horseflies were still eating his eyeballs when we found it. Came across the guy's body later. He'd been lucky compared to his partner. The Yaqui had cut him up so bad he didn't really have a face left. Ears, nose, lips and eyes had all been sliced away. They'd also built a fire at his crotch. Didn't have much left there either.''

"Jesus," the young bounty hunter muttered. "They sound like demons right outta hell."

"The Yaqui could scare the shit out of demons," Clint replied. "And any *bandido* gang that can hide out in the Devil's Belly has to be even worse than the Yaqui."

"Kinda makes a feller wonder if he made the wrong choice about accepting this job," Collins said.

"Too late for that now," Moonlance grunted.

"Well," the Gunsmith said, "if we keep going, it won't get any easier. If either of you want to back out, better do it now."

"Let's go, Clint," Collins declared firmly.

The trio continued into the formidable, barren desert. The heat felt like an open blast furnace. Sunlight seemed to flash against the sand as if it were polished glass.

"Christ," Moonlance growled as he shielded his eyes with a palm. "Is the whole desert like this?"

"No," the Gunsmith replied. "It gets worse."

"I see some rock formations up ahead," Collins announced, squinting his eyes. "Looks like a perfect spot for an ambush to me."

"Heads up, gents," Clint warned as he reached for the Springfield carbine in a saddle boot. "Better expect trouble."

Moonlance followed Clint's example and drew his Winchester from its scabbard. They approached the rocks slowly. The stony monuments towered above them on both sides. All three men tensed, ready to spring into action at the first sign of trouble.

Then the Gunsmith saw the glint of sunlight against

gunmetal among the rocks. He responded instantly, bringing the stock of his Springfield to his shoulder. Clint located the bearded face of a sniper through the sights of his carbine. The drygulcher's rifle was already aimed at the Gunsmith.

Clint triggered his weapon first. A .45-caliber slug smashed into the sniper's face. His nose vanished and his sombrero hopped into the air as his skull burst into a crimson nova. The rifleman dropped his weapon and slid against the rockwall in a lifeless lump.

More figures appeared among the stone towers. The ambushers wore the unofficial uniform of *bandidos*. Their clothes were ill-treated and filthy. Sombreros with shapeless brims capped their shaggy heads. Bandoliers of ammunition crisscrossed their chests and weapons hung from their belts like savage ornaments.

"Down!" the Gunsmith shouted as he leaped from Duke's back.

Clint hit the ground and tumbled into a fast forward roll. Half a dozen guns roared. Bullets slashed into sand within inches of Clint's hurtling figure. The Gunsmith rolled twice, working the lever of his carbine at the same time. He assumed a prone position, Springfield braced to a shoulder.

The front sight bisected the chest of a *bandido*. Clint fired his weapon. The bandit howled and recoiled violently when a bullet ripped through his torso. The man plunged headlong over the lip of a rock ledge. He crashed to earth forty feet below.

Moonlance shot another opponent with his Winchester. A third *bandido* screamed and fell from the boulders. Clint glanced about to see Collins draw a revolver from leather.

"Put that pistol away until they're closer!" the Gunsmith shouted at the young bounty hunter. "Use your rifle, Collins!"

Another bullet struck sand near Clint. The Gunsmith rolled to a new position behind the cover of a boulder. He jacked a fresh round into the breech of his Springfield.

"Oh, shit," Clint rasped when he saw more than a dozen bandits shuffling across the rock walls.

Clint opened fire. A fourth *bandido* cried out in agony before he took a bone-shattering swan dive to the ground. Clint glanced about to see Duke bolt for the shelter of another rock formation. Moonlance had dismounted and continued to fire his rifle at the ambushers. Collins remained on horseback and still held his pistol in his fist as he galloped toward the Gunsmith's position.

"Get off that horse, you idiot!" Clint yelled at the younger man.

Two bullets chipped stone from Clint's cover. The Gunsmith worked the lever of his carbine and swung the weapon in the direction of the enemy. He quickly took aim as two bandits jogged forward.

Something hit the side of Clint's skull, splitting skin and burning into muscle and nerves. The Gunsmith's head was propelled into the surface of the boulder. He felt a burst of white hot pain before a black veil fell over him. The universe vanished and Clint Adams plunged into a bottomless pit.

EIGHT

The Gunsmith's skull throbbed with pain. He stifled a groan. Instinct warned him to take care. Whoever had knocked him unconscious might still be around.

He did not open his eyes. The Gunsmith felt gritty hot sand under his face and hands. He tried to ignore the pain which became steadily worse as his senses returned. He listened for any sound which might indicate danger or tell him about his present environment.

Memories of recent events gradually returned as his head cleared. The sun pounded down on Clint. Sweat poured from his skin and plastered the denim shirt to his back. Clint still waited, listening.

The Gunsmith heard nothing except the throb of a pulse behind his ear. Gradually, he opened his eyes. The base of a boulder towered over him like a headstone.

He slowly turned his head to stare out at the clearing where the gunfight had taken place. Several bodies littered the ground. Clint still heard no voices or even a groan to suggest any living thing was in the area.

An angry shriek suddenly broke the silence. The Gunsmith automatically reached for his Colt revolver. His hand clutched air above an empty holster. Another scream pierced his ears. It was a hideous sound, shrill and inhuman.

Indeed, the voice did not belong to a person. Clint saw two ugly squat figures hopping about near one of the corpses. The creatures flapped their great black wings and opened curved beaks, trying to frighten each other with an exaggerated show of ferocity.

"Goddamn vultures," the Gunsmith muttered as he grasped the boulder for support and rose to his feet.

Clint knew he couldn't lie still and rest with the scavengers in the area. Vultures prey on the dead, but they don't check for a pulse before they start to use their beaks. If Clint passed out, he might not wake up until a buzzard had plucked out one of his eyeballs for a snack.

The Gunsmith staggered forward. The presence of a live creature startled the birds. The vultures cried out in fear and indignation. They bolted into the sky with a burst of flapping feathers. Clint braced himself against the rocks and gazed down at the dead.

He counted half a dozen corpses. Joe Moonlance lay sprawled on his back. Three gory bullet holes had been gouged into his chest. The other bodies were slain *bandidos*. Clint look around again. No sign of Stark Collins—dead or alive.

"Little bastard," Clint rasped, touching a patch of dried blood on the side of his head.

The Gunsmith remembered that he was facing the

bandits when he had been shot. The bullet struck from behind. Clint had turned his back to Stark Collins just before the lead slug creased his skull.

"Collins," he hissed. "Son of a bitch must have been working for Gila all along."

Clint cursed under his breath, furious that he'd allowed himself to be taken out by a punk like Collins. The Gunsmith recalled how the young bounty hunter had pretended to be so naive and concerned about the morality of robbing from the dead or burying Manuel Sharp in Mexico. Clint had suspected Collins was acting, but he hadn't guessed the kid was one of Gila's men.

The Gunsmith had committed the ultimate sin. He had underestimated his enemy. Gila was more clever and better organized than he had thought the *bandido* was capable of being. Clint had been careless. His poor judgment concerning Gila and Collins had almost cost him his life.

Clint gingerly examined the crusty stain of dried blood stuck to the side of his head. The bullet had split flesh just above his left temple. It would have been fatal had the projectile struck less than an inch lower or to the right.

The bandits had obviously assumed Clint was dead. They certainly hadn't been wrong about any of the others left behind. The Gunsmith checked the bodies to be certain all of them were dead. Moonlance and the slain *bandidos* proved to be as lifeless as the rocks which surrounded them.

Clint found a small patch of shade and sat down in it, resting his back against a boulder. His head still ached and his stomach felt as if it was tumbling inside his belly. Looking at those corpses hadn't helped. One of the bandits had already been mutilated by the hungry vultures before Clint frightened the birds away.

He tried to relax in order to evaluate the circumstances as calmly as possible. The situation appeared to be somewhere between extremely desperate and utterly hopeless.

The enemy had taken Clint's Springfield carbine and his double-action Colt. He had checked the corpses for weapons, but hadn't found a single firearm or even a sheath knife. However, the Gunsmith still had his holdout "belly gun" tucked inside his belt under his shirt.

The backup piece was a diminutive .22-caliber New Line Colt revolver. It hardly qualified as a proper combat weapon, but the little pistol had saved Clint's life more than once. Still, he didn't feel properly armed with only a small caliber, short-range weapon in his possession.

The Gunsmith whistled sharply and called out for Duke. The black gelding did not respond. Clint cursed bitterly. The bastards had taken Duke as well.

This meant all the supplies in his saddlebags were gone too. Including his water. None of the slain bandits had canteens either. A hell of a situation for a man on foot in the desert.

Clint rose. He drew the .22 New Line from his shirt and thrust it into his belt where it would be more readily available. Then he staggered forward to examine the hoofprints left by the *bandidos*.

There seemed to be only one choice of action. Clint would have to follow the gang's tracks and hope he could survive long enough to catch up with the bastards.

What would he do when he found them?

The Gunsmith would handle that problem when the time came.

Clint Adams shuffled across the sand slowly. He had draped his neckerchief over his head to form a curtain over the back of his neck and covered it with his stetson. The Gunsmith realized the danger of heat stroke. The desert sun could suck a man's body fluids dry.

He had also smeared some dirt on his lower eyelids to protect against the glare of the sun. Clint paced himself carefully, aware that he'd tire rapidly in the merciless heat. If he pushed himself too much, the desert would kill him as surely as a bullet.

The Gunsmith followed the trail of the bandit gang. He tracked the hoofprints across the barren terrain for hours until exhaustion forced him to rest. He gazed about the bleak surroundings in search of shade. There were no rocks or boulders available now. The only shadow in the area was his own.

Then Clint noticed a lump of sand in the distance. The desert island attracted him like a moth to a lantern. Such raised sections often mean an underground stream in the desert.

The Gunsmith staggered to the mound. He fell to his knees before it and clawed at the sand with his fingers. Clint used his hands for shovels. He dug deeper, but found no trace of moisture.

Clint moved to a different position and tried again. His hands raked away sand. He thrust his fingers into the ground and found the soft texture of mud. The Gunsmith dug deeper. The tiny hole suddenly filled with dark murky water.

He used his neckerchief to soak up the water. Clint held the cloth high and tilted back his head. He squeezed the bandanna to pour the precious liquid into his open mouth. The water was gritty, foul and bitter. Yet he welcomed it.

Although Clint realized the water might be tainted or toxic, he also knew that he'd die without more fluid in his system. Thus he accepted the risk. The Gunsmith repeated the procedure and drank as much of the muddy liquid as he could soak up from the hole.

The Gunsmith moved to a new position and once again dug at the base of the mound. His fingers clawed away more sand. Then something darted across the back of his right hand. Tiny feet scrambled up his arm. Clint glanced down at a sleek shape with tiny pincers poised in front of an ugly set of mandibles. The creature's whiplike tail rose and prepared to strike.

Clint gasped in horror and swiftly swatted the scorpion off his sleeve before it could use its stinger. Movement burst from the sandy hole Clint had begun to dig. Half a dozen scorpions scurried from the earth. The Gunsmith recoiled from the charging swarm of poisonous arachnids. He fell into a fast roll and tumbled away from the mound.

"Jesus," Clint rasped breathlessly as he watched the scorpions scramble about like miniature demons on leave from Hades. "Everything in this goddamn desert is trying to kill me."

NINE

Clint followed the *bandidos'* trail until the sun slid into the horizon. The Gunsmith was many things, but he was not an expert tracker. Even a professional adept at reading sign has great difficulty tracking in the dark. Clint realized that trying to do so would probably get him even more lost.

The Gunsmith located two cone-shaped boulders and huddled down between them. There was a little sagebrush available, but no greasewood or tumbleweeds for a fire. The temperature in the desert after sundown can drop dramatically from sizzling hot to bitter cold. Clint had no blankets or spare clothes.

The only protection from the elements was to remain between the two large stones for shelter from the wind. The Gunsmith removed the mud-stained bandanna and wiped some grime from his neck with a palm. Clint clucked his tongue, disgusted by his own filth. He wiped the mud on his Levi's.

"Great mess you got yourself into," Clint muttered to himself.

He tried to get comfortable and chewed some sagebrush leaves. His stomach rumbled unhappily. Clint told it to shut up. He allowed himself a few minutes of fantasies about catching up with Gila's band and getting revenge.

Since he'd developed a greater resentment toward Collins's treachery than the rest of the outlaws, his primary target for retribution was the young bounty hunter. The Gunsmith imagined shooting him in the gut and watching him thrash about in agony, begging to be put out of his misery, or maybe he'd shoot Stark Collins through both kneecaps and elbows and leave him lying helpless in the desert.

Of course Clint wouldn't carry out such brutality. He wasn't that sort of man. Fighting a man on even terms was the Gunsmith's style. Not murder or torture. Yet if those bastards had harmed Duke, Clint might just revise that attitude.

Clint watched the sunset and enjoyed a cool breeze which stroked his sunburned skin like a gentle balm. Exhausted muscles relaxed and the Gunsmith closed his eyes in slumber.

The temperature continued to drop until Clint awoke with a violent shudder. Sweat seemed to freeze against his flesh. The chill bit into muscles and nerves. The wind roared like a vicious beast, an arctic demon which breathed a burning fire of ice.

"Never figured I'd die of pneumonia," Clint rasped through chattering teeth. "Hell, that's almost natural causes."

Freezing to death in a desert wasn't exactly a natural cause, but it was becoming quite a likely one. Clint felt as if his bones were being lanced by needles of ice. He curled into a ball, trying to find some warmth within his own body.

The Gunsmith wished Captain Foster was there. He'd tell the Texas Ranger to keep his goddamn money. Clint would have given the whole four thousand dollars to have a single flea-infested horse blanket.

He needed something to cover his body from the terrible frosty wind. There were no cottonwood trees with leafy branches to build a lean-to. The sagebrush was too sparse to improvise as a blanket. Far from stopping the cold, the boulders seemed to have been transformed into a pair of ice blocks by the cruel desert night.

Clint squirmed against the sand, hoping movement and friction would help warm his tortured body. Suddenly he realized he was surrounded by a substance that could help protect his vulnerable flesh. The Gunsmith clawed at the ground, he scooping out handfuls of dirt like a mole digging a burrow.

At last he'd dug a shallow pit, six feet long and two feet deep. The Gunsmith lay down in the ditch and pulled the sand over his feet and legs. He slipped the New Line Colt inside his shirt to keep it from getting filled with dirt before he pawed more sand over his torso.

Eventually Clint was all but covered with sand. The cold still stroked his skin, but only a subdued chill managed to penetrate the blanket of sand. With the worst effects of the wind at last defeated, Clint Adams canted his stetson over his face and once again drifted into sleep.

● ● ●

When the Gunsmith awoke at dawn, it felt strange to sit up in the gravelike hole. The sensation of being buried alive was uncomfortable to say the least.

After he'd dusted himself off he took out the little belly gun, unloaded and disassembled it and cleaned it as best he could to be certain sand didn't clog the barrel or cylinder. The Gunsmith put the pistol back together and loaded it.

Clint chewed some sagebrush, trying to convince his empty stomach to be patient. He stretched stiff muscles and walked to the tracks left by the *bandidos'* horses. Clint knelt by the trail and studied the prints. The wind had swept sand across the tracks, but it hadn't obliterated them.

Suddenly an object hissed down from the sky, slicing air inches from Clint's face. He immediately jumped back in alarm. The wooden shaft of an arrow jutted from the ground near his feet.

A savage war whoop erupted behind the Gunsmith. He whirled, clawing for the New Line Colt in his belt as he turned to face his assailants. Three Yaqui Indian braves snarled at him like a trio of rabid wolves.

The Yaqui were small, wiry men dressed only in ragged loincloths and armed with primitive weapons. Yet they were a deadly, brutal breed, hardened by life in a hostile environment. Their hatred for outsiders dated back to the *conquistadores*. They had suffered under the Spanish and been oppressed by the Mexican government for decades. Every advanced culture had treated the Indians with contempt. Long ago they had been driven into the deserts. Their ancestors had been introduced to the fine points of torture by advocates of the Holy Inquisition among the Spanish. The Yaqui had learned that outsiders were the enemy and deserved no mercy.

However, Clint didn't have time to consider the motives of the three men who attacked him. There was only one rule in the Devil's Belly: Survive.

Only one Indian was armed with a bow. Another carried a crude war lance and the third wielded a tomahawk with a sharp stone head. The archer notched another arrow to the string of his bow while the others charged.

The Yaqui's spindly little bow gave him a greater range than Clint's short-barreled belly gun. He held his fire and waited for the Indians to close in.

The archer let loose a second arrow. The Gunsmith threw himself to the ground and the missile sailed harmlessly above his hurtling form. Before Clint could rise, another Yaqui closed in and thrust his spear at the Gunsmith's chest.

Clint shifted to the right. The flint blade of the lance struck earth next to the Gunsmith's thigh. He raised his New Line Colt and triggered the tiny handgun. A .22-caliber bullet hit the Yaqui lancer under the nose.

The lancer dropped dead in the blink of an eye, but his ax-wielding partner had also closed in and swung his tomahawk at the Gunsmith's head. The stone blade missed its intended target, but the wooden shaft struck Clint's right wrist. The blow jarred the ulna nerve in his arm and knocked the New Line from Clint's grasp.

The Yaqui drew back his axe for another attack. Clint lashed a boot upward and kicked the Indian between his splayed legs. The brave bellowed and doubled up in agony. Such a punishing kick to the testicles would have put most men out of action, but the tough Yaqui hissed in anger and swung his stone ax in a fast cross-body stroke.

The Gunsmith lunged forward and grabbed the Indian's forearm with both hands. He pulled hard, nearly yanking the Yaqui off balance. The brave kept his footing, but suddenly screamed and convulsed in agony.

Clint twisted the man's arm. The tomahawk fell to the ground. Then the Yaqui himself crashed face first to the sand. The slender shaft of an arrow vibrated between his shoulder blades. The archer had claimed the wrong victim.

The last Yaqui rushed forward and tossed his bow aside. He had clearly used his last arrow and thus eagerly reached for another weapon. The Indian scooped up his comrade's war lance while the Gunsmith grabbed the stone ax. The Gunsmith rose to his feet as the Yaqui lunged with his spear.

Clint's left hand flashed and hurled a fistful of sand at the Indian's face. Stinging grains flew into the man's open eyes and mouth. Half blind, his lance thrust missed its mark. Clint dodged the blade and swung the tomahawk with all his might.

The stone ax struck the Yaqui warrior on top of the head and his skull cracked like an eggshell against the rim of an iron skillet.

"Shit," the Gunsmith gasped as he sank to his knees beside the slain Yaqui. "I hate this fucking place."

TEN

The rattlesnake's tail quivered, signaling a warning to the human invader. The Gunsmith would have heeded the rattle under other conditions, but the serpent was the first source of food he'd encountered for a day and a half.

"You or me, snake," Clint Adams whispered as he approached the reptile with the Yaqui lance held in his fists.

The rattler raised its head and opened its jaws to display a large pair of impressive curved fangs. Clint poked the spear at the snake. It reacted swiftly and struck at the shaft.

The Gunsmith twisted his wrists to swing the lance in a short, fast arch. The sharp flint blade caught the serpent at the back of its neck. Clint chopped down hard. The snake's head popped from its body.

"Sorry, fella," the Gunsmith muttered. "Nothing personal, but I gotta eat."

He used the lance to shove the serpent's head away, aware that even severed from its body, a rattlesnake can still bite by reflex. Clint watched the decapitated body thrash about on the ground until the last traces of movement ceased.

He used the lance blade to slit open the belly of the snake. The reptile's scaly hide was tough and its muscular development incredible. But Clint was determined and managed to cut the serpent open.

He scooped out its guts and organs with his fingers, then he stripped off the skin and pulled out chunks of meat which he ate raw.

"Could have used a little more salt," he muttered sourly, yet the snake had tasted better than he would have expected.

Clint rested for a few minutes before he continued to track the bandits' trail. The Gunsmith used the Yaqui lance for a stave as he walked. The stone ax and the .22 Colt were thrust in his belt. He felt like a throwback to a prehistoric era.

Perhaps this was the only attitude which would allow one to survive in a place like the Devil's Belly.

The Gunsmith followed the bandits' tracks to a small village. It resembled Grajo, yet Clint recognized the adobe houses and modest church. Two years before he had arrived at the tiny hamlet of San José and had found friendship and love.

"My God," Clint whispered in astonishment. "The bastards hit San José."

He hurried toward the village. As he drew closer the Gunsmith was relieved to see *peónes* moving about. There were no *bandidos* in view. If Gila's gang had passed through, at least they hadn't slaughtered the population.

The villagers noticed Clint. Unlike most *peónes*, the men of San José did not flee to their homes and hide. Two figures appeared holding rifles. They waited for Clint to get closer and then shouted something in Spanish. Clint wasn't sure what they said, but it sounded more like a warning than a welcome.

"I'm a friend," Clint assured them. "*Yo soy amigo. Comprende?*"

"What do you want, *señor?*" a large, husky man demanded in broken English.

"My name is Clint Adams," the Gunsmith replied. "I want to talk to you and ask for what help you can give."

"Clint Adams?" The big man's voice revealed surprise. "I have heard much about you . . . if indeed you are the Gunsmith. Come forward, but keep your hands where I can see them."

The Gunsmith obliged. He tossed the Yaqui war lance aside and walked toward the village with both hands held high. The large man waited for Clint while another *péon* dashed into the church.

"My name is Julio Veaga," the big man explained, holding his rifle at port arms. "I was a *federale* sergeant at Fort Juarez before I decided to marry a girl from this village. Now I live here. I warn you, I was trained to use guns. I will do so if I must." Veaga did not look or act like a *peón*. He was more than six feet tall and built like a black bear. With his dense black beard and snoutlike nose the ex-*federale* even resembled a bear.

"I don't want to fight you," Clint assured him. "I told you, I'm a friend."

"So you say." Veaga shrugged. "I did not live in San José when the Gunsmith helped the people of this village against el Espectro's *bandidos*, but they still speak of it often. Clint Adams is a great hero to these people. It will go badly for you if you aren't the Gunsmith and claim to be him.''

"Let me talk to Father Rameriz," Clint told him.

"I am here, my son," a gentle voice announced.

The Gunsmith turned to see a figure dressed in a brown robe. The priest used a stave to test each step as he moved his feet forward. A smile appeared on his round face. Rameriz's eyes were colorless with milky pupils, yet his sightless orbs somehow conveyed as much warmth and friendship as the expression on his lips.

"We hoped one day you would return, Clint," the priest said as he shuffled toward the Gunsmith. "Welcome back, my son."

ELEVEN

Father Rameriz and Clint Adams sat at a table in the priest's chamber within the church. On the table between them was a hand-carved chess set which the priest had made before his vision had faded. The pieces featured raised symbols which allowed Rameriz to identify the chessmen by touch. Every other square of the board was also raised so Rameriz could feel the surface when he moved a piece.

In many ways Father Rameriz was a very impressive man. The priest was a well-read scholar and linguist who spoke four languages fluently. Clint admired Rameriz's dedication to the people of San José and his courage in the face of danger.

It was very good to meet the priest again.

"Would you care for some more wine, my son?" Rameriz inquired as he gestured toward a bottle and two glasses next to the chess set.

"Not right now, Father," the Gunsmith replied. "I

61

appreciate your hospitality more than I can say.''

Clint had been warmly received by the priest and the other residents of San José. The Gunsmith was given food and drink. He enjoyed the wonderful luxury of a hot bath and happily washed the mud and grime from his weary body.

The Gunsmith was given a clean pair of cotton trousers and a peasant shirt until his old clothes could be washed. He felt as if he'd been resurrected.

"It would be un-Christian to deny aid to a man in need," Rameriz said. "This village owes a debt to you, my son. We're happy to be able to do whatever we can for you.''

"The people of San José don't owe me anything,'' Clint assured him.

"We feel differently,'' the blind man said. "But you did not come to San José simply to visit us.''

"No.''

"And I was told you arrived on foot,'' Rameriz remarked. "You did not cross the desert without a horse unless you were forced to do so.''

Clint nodded. "That's a fact.''

He told the priest why he was in Mexico and how he had been stranded in the desert. Rameriz frowned as he listened to Clint's tale.

"So you are once again chasing another *bandido* gang across Mexico,'' he commented. "You need a new hobby, my son. This one is too dangerous.''

Clint shrugged. "I'm really just a traveling gunsmith by trade. But I get sort of sidetracked from time to time.''

"How old are you, Clint?'' the priest asked. "Thirty? Thirty-five?''

"A few years older than that," the Gunsmith confessed. "Why?"

"How long do you think you can continue taking such risks?" Rameriz inquired as he reached for the wine bottle. "When are you going to settle down, get married and raise a family?"

"When are you going to do those things, Father?" Clint Adams asked with a grin.

"I am a priest," Rameriz said solemnly. "My duty to God includes a vow of celibacy. This is hardly true in your case, is it, my son?"

The Gunsmith grinned. "Not exactly. Reckon my life-style isn't much like yours. But don't expect me to apologize for it, Father."

"I wouldn't ask you to, Clint. How you live your life is up to you," Rameriz said as he carefully poured some wine into a glass. "I did not mean to lecture you."

"No offense taken, Father," the Gunsmith assured him. "But we'd better concentrate on Gila and forget about my sinful ways for now."

"We are all sinners," Rameriz remarked, "but Gila is a demon in human form."

"He can't be any worse than el Espectro," Clint mused.

"I don't think he's any better than the Ghost was," the priest replied as he sipped his wine. "Although Gila has not made our village as miserable as el Espectro did in the past."

"I'm not surprised," Clint said. "Some of your people have guns now. Bandits don't like to tangle with anybody who can shoot back at them."

"Gila's gang isn't worried by a handful of *peónes*

with guns. The bandits realize they're more than a match for this village."

"So he's been to San José more than once," Clint remarked.

"*Sí*," the priest confirmed. "The first time was two months ago. The bandits demanded food and other supplies. One of the men of our village told him we'd be happy to sell the group what we could afford to part with from our supplies. Gila found this quite amusing. He was still laughing when he shot the young man through the heart."

"Your people should have killed Gila on the spot," Clint stated.

"Two of them tried," Rameriz declared. "One farmer aimed his gun at Gila, but the other bandits shot him down before he could use it. The third man, however, managed to fire his pistol. Those who saw this incident claim he shot Gila in the center of the chest. I heard a sound which may have been a bullet striking his breastplate."

"You mean that thing really stopped a bullet?" Clint scoffed. "Come on, Father. Anything that heavy would be impossible to wear in the middle of a desert. The heat inside that armor would boil Gila like a New England lobster."

"Yet he still lives, no?" The priest shrugged. "The bandits killed the third farmer as well. Gila laughed and dared the other villagers to try to kill him if they wanted to. No one accepted this challenge. The bandits took what they wanted and rode on. We could only bury our dead and pray the gang would not return."

"But they did."

"Twice more. No one wants to die, Clint. Thus no

one opposed Gila when he demanded supplies again.
Since the *bandidos* could easily destroy the village, we
had little choice but to agree to their demands.''

"Why do you say Gila isn't as bad as the Ghost?
Sounds like he's doing the same sort of crap to your
people.''

"Gila has not kidnapped any of our people as el
Espectro did," Rameriz explained. "And he has not
killed any of them since that first day when we opposed
him.''

"He's just terrorized your people and forced them
to pay tribute to him as if he was a warlord." Clint
clucked his tongue with disgust. "I'd hoped the villagers would be able to defend themselves after that
business with el Espectro.''

"The villagers thought they could handle *bandidos*," Rameriz replied. "But their guns failed them
when they tried to fight Gila. They have lost their spirit
to fight again.''

"Guns aren't magic sticks that go boom," Clint
said. "They're tools like a hoe or a shovel.''

"Guns are weapons," the priest stated. "They are
made not for work, but to kill.''

"That depends on how you look at things," Clint
said. "You can use a gun to either take life or save life.
Your people might have been able to defend themselves against the bandits if they knew how to use
firearms properly. But they figured just owning a gun
would protect them. They had a false sense of security.
Figured they'd just have to wave a gun and the bad
guys would run away. When they tried it, the bluff
didn't work because the bandits didn't hesitate to shoot
back.''

"But they used their guns," Rameriz insisted. "They didn't just wave them and utter false threats. Shooting at Gila's men did not work."

"One man fired one shot at Gila," Clint stated. "One lousy shot. When that failed your people fell apart instead of sticking together and fighting."

"Perhaps," the priest allowed. "But I don't think even you can convince them to fight now. They are more concerned with protecting their own lives and their families than they are about paying tribute to Gila."

"They fought bravely against el Espectro."

"Only because their backs were to the wall. They had no choice except to fight because el Espectro intended to kill them all."

"They had nothing to lose by fighting back," Clint agreed. "Gila hasn't given them ample reason to feel that desperate . . . *yet*. Still, Julio Veaga sure seems ready to fight if he has to."

"*Sí*," the priest agreed. "Julio was not a farmer until he joined this community six months ago. He is not a *peón* and he would happily take on Gila if he did not realize he couldn't do this alone."

"Too bad you don't have more men like him in this village."

"Don't condemn my people because they are afraid, Clint. Everyone fears something—although, I must confess, I have no idea what frightens you."

"A lot of things do," the Gunsmith assured him. "But I try not to let fear prevent me from taking action when it has to be done. Tell me what happened when Gila and his band rode into San José yesterday."

"Not much to tell," the blind man answered. "The

bandidos wanted some food and water. We gave it to them. The bandits dismounted and rested for a while. A few of them even came into the church to pray. Two *bandidos* made confessions to me.''

"I bet they gave you an earful,'' Clint mused.

"To say the least,'' Rameriz confirmed. "After they ate and rested, the gang rode on. No one was hurt. We were thankful their visit remained peaceful.''

"I've got to go after those sons of bitches, Father.''

"It's getting late, my son,'' the priest told him. "You need to rest. Sleep here, in my chamber. Tomorrow you can continue your hunt for vengeance.''

"That's a fact,'' Clint agreed.

TWELVE

The Gunsmith lay on a cot with a blanket over his weary body. It may not have been as comfortable as a feather bed, but it was sure better than sleeping half-buried in the sand between two boulders. Twilight had fallen and darkness filled the church. Clint drifted into a deep, dreamless sleep.

His slumber was interrupted by a faint sound, a whisper of noise, too slight to penetrate his exhausted senses or trigger his battle-honed reflexes. Yet, his subconscious detected the sound and it served to manufacture a dream within his resting mind.

Clint felt vulnerable in the dream. He lay strapped to a table or a torture rack. The Gunsmith glanced about the dark room of his illusion, but saw nothing except shadows. Then a door creaked open and a figure entered the dungeon. Clint saw the ominous, distorted black shape, yet he could not recognize features or even be certain of the sex of his intruder. He wasn't even sure it was human.

"Clint," a voice whispered. "Can you hear me?"

The Gunsmith awoke with a start. His eyes snapped open to find himself in a dark room not unlike the one in his dream. A black figure towered over him. He saw a head and shoulders and a hand which moved toward his face.

Clint reacted swiftly. His left arm rose to ward off the attack. His right hand reached for the twenty-two New Line on the floor beside the cot.

"Clint!" a woman's voice gasped in alarm. "Don't be upset. It is I. Elena."

"Elena." The Gunsmith blinked and sat up. "Elena, it really is you."

"Of course, my darling," she whispered. "At last we are together again."

Clint Adams recalled how he had first met Elena Jimenez. The Gunsmith was traveling through el Barriga del Diablo with a *bandido* captive for an unwilling guide. Suddenly, a girl ran into view, a beautiful young woman with a slender body and big, soft eyes which conveyed emotions openly.

Elena was as courageous as she was beautiful. The girl had helped Clint fight el Espectro and his formidable gang.

When Clint had said farewell to Elena two years ago, she told him that somehow they would meet again. Their parting had not been *adiós* but *hasta mañana*—until tomorrow.

Tomorrow had at last arrived.

Elena cupped Clint's face in her hands and lowered her mouth to his. They kissed slowly, gently, and gradually pressed their lips together harder. Tongues probed inside mouths with eager passion.

The girl stroked Clint's chest and belly, running her hands over his loose-fitting shirt. The Gunsmith fondled Elena's breasts and gently thumbed her nipples. She cooed with pleasure and reached down to caress Clint's crotch.

Clint climbed from the cot while the girl slipped out of her peasant dress. The Gunsmith followed her example and began to strip off his clothes as well. Soon they were both naked.

They embraced, flesh touching flesh, fingers stroking warm skin. Clint kissed the girl's throat. Elena gripped his pulsating cock and slowly caressed it.

They practically tumbled together to the floor. Elena sprawled on her back, spread her legs widely apart and guided his hard member home.

The Gunsmith turned his hips slightly as he slowly worked himself deeper. The girl moaned happily as he increased his thrusts, faster and harder until the girl exploded in an erotic spasm. The Gunsmith controlled his own passion and gradually repeated the procedure until Elena once again trembled in joy. Clint then lunged with unfettered passion.

Elena cried out as she wrapped her strong, shapely legs around his hips. Clint burst inside her as the girl convulsed with the glory of her third orgasm.

"I dreamed of your return," Elena whispered. "I had given up hope that I would see you again. I simply had to come here and make love to you tonight. I know it was wrong . . ."

"I'm glad you came," the Gunsmith assured her, holding the girl gently in his arms.

"But I should not have done this," the girl said, tears forming in her large, dark eyes.

"What's wrong, Elena?" Clint asked, surprised by her outburst. "You haven't done anything—"

"*Que la chigada!*" a voice snarled.

The Gunsmith glanced up to see a figure dressed in white cotton shirt and trousers materialize from the darkness. Clint pulled away from Elena and leaped to his feet as the assailant closed in rapidly. A long, curved blade flashed in the attacker's fist.

"*Bastardo!*" the assailant exclaimed. "I'm going to rip out your testicles and feed them to you, *gringo*!"

The sickle slashed at the Gunsmith; he dodged the whirling blade, then hissed with pain as the sharp steel sliced through flesh. Warm blood oozed from the shallow wound in his left thigh.

The Gunsmith grabbed the arm behind the sickle before the killer could swing the long blade again. Clint clenched the man's wrist in his right hand and punched his left fist into the aggressor's face. Then he seized the arm with both hands and shoved down hard to hammer the killer's limb across a bent knee.

The sickle fell from the assassin's numb fingers. Clint heard his opponent groan in pain. He lashed another left hook to his adversary's face. The man staggered backward from the punch. Clint followed him and swung a right cross.

The assailant blocked the punch with a forearm. Clint felt knuckles crash into his own jaw. With a bellow of rage, the attacker pounced forward and grabbed Clint's throat with one hand while the other clawed at the Gunsmith's crotch.

Clint's left hand caught the man's wrist to keep his

fingernails from tearing into his testicles. The Gunsmith's right fist hammered the killer's other wrist to break the grip from his throat. Before the attacker could recover from Clint's move, the Gunsmith quickly butted his forehead into the man's face.

The assailant stumbled from the blow. Clint swung a solid right to the killer's jaw. The man's head recoiled and his knees buckled as he began to sag. The Gunsmith lunged forward and whipped a knee between his opponent's splayed legs.

"No!" Elena cried. "Stop! *Por favor!*"

Clint's adversary began to crumple to the floor, but the Gunsmith didn't intend to take any chances with the man. He grabbed the killer's hair in his left fist and raised his head to slam a powerful right cross to the point of his assailant's jaw. The aggressor crashed to the floor hard.

"Raul?" Elena exclaimed as she knelt beside the fallen man.

"What the hell?" Clint Adams muttered. "You know this guy, Elena?"

"*Sí,*" she confirmed sadly. "He is Raul Medoza . . . my husband."

THIRTEEN

"Husband?" The Gunsmith glared at Elena. "So that's why you felt guilty about making love to me."

"Please, Clint," she began, still kneeling by Raul. "Let me explain."

"Explain it to your husband," Clint told her gruffly as he pulled on his trousers. "He's the one you've wronged."

"Clint!" the voice of Father Rameriz called out. "Are you all right, my son?"

"Yeah," the Gunsmith replied. "Just had a misunderstanding with a couple of the locals."

"A physical misunderstanding," the priest said as he entered the chamber. "I recognized the sound of a fight."

"I'm sorry, Father," Clint said. "I've abused your hospitality."

"It wasn't your fault, Clint," Elena declared. "I am to blame, Father."

"Yeah," the Gunsmith muttered. "Reckon you are at that."

"Blame is not important now," Rameriz said as he shuffled forward, moving easily through the shadows. "I hear a third person breathing hard. Is this Raul?"

"*Sí*, Father," Elena admitted, her voice choked by emotion. "My husband is just regaining consciousness."

"Let me help him, my child," Rameriz said as he approached.

Raul suddenly pushed his wife violently aside. She cried out in alarm and fell to the floor. The young farmer rose up quickly, but his knees buckled and he dropped to all fours. Raul gasped and shook his head, trying to clear it.

"Slowly, my son," Rameriz urged, placing a hand on Raul's shoulder. "And think before you get up. There have been enough hasty actions tonight."

"This *gringo* took my wife, Father," Raul rasped. "He had her right here in your chambers. Can you condone such sacrilege?"

"And you tried to kill Clint, no?" the priest inquired. "Do you think murder in the house of God is more acceptable than fornication?"

"*Adultery*, Father," Raul corrected. "Elena is my wife. This *gringo* is—"

"Is my guest, Raul," Rameriz insisted. "You will not commit any more acts of violence against him."

"Not inside your church, Father," the farmer agreed.

"Raul," Elena began, "I know I have wronged you, but—"

"*Calla te, puta*," Raul snapped. "Do not speak to me again, you slut."

The young *peón* stormed out of the chamber. Elena burst into tears and chased after her husband. The Gunsmith watched the two figures dash through the shadows beyond the chamber. Father Rameriz shook his head sadly.

"Such a pity," the priest sighed. "Such a pity."

FOURTEEN

The following morning, Father Rameriz assembled the people of San José in front of the church. He spoke to the congregation in Spanish on Clint's behalf. Clint wanted a gun, a horse and some supplies. That was all he would ask of the people of San José . . . and he'd be surprised if they could grant him that much. Thus he was startled when Julio Veaga stepped forward.

"I will go with *Señor* Adams," the big man announced. "We will track down Gila and his *bandidos* together."

"I can't allow you to . . ." Clint began.

"It is not your decision to make, *señor.*" Veaga smiled. "I want to go. I want to fight these murderous scum."

"Look," the Gunsmith said, "I don't want to endanger anyone else."

"I have heard you are a very brave man, *señor,*"

Veaga said. "But I am brave too. We will go together."

"I need a gun and a horse more than a partner," Clint said bluntly.

"We can give you a gun," Father Rameriz stated. "But we have no horses. You'll have to settle for a mule."

"A mule?" the Gunsmith groaned. "Well, it beats trying to cross the desert on foot. What kind of gun do I get?"

"A forty-four-caliber Remington revolver," Veaga answered as he offered the pistol, butt first, to Clint. "Pulls a little to the right."

"I wish there was time to get a little practice with this thing first," Clint mused as he inspected the revolver. "Probably can't spare the ammunition anyway. Thanks for the gun, *Señor* Veaga."

"Call me Julio."

"And my name is Clint. Are you sure you want to do this, my friend?"

"*Sí,*" Veaga smiled. "There is nothing I'd like better than to see Gila and his men lying dead at my feet."

"I will also go with the Gunsmith," another man declared.

Clint recognized the voice. It belonged to a young farmer who stepped forward to stand beside Veaga. He was medium height and build, with a handsome lean face. A dark purple bruise marred the corner of his jaw.

"No, Raul," Father Rameriz told him. "You must certainly realize that is impossible."

"Everyone believes Adams is such a brave man," Raul snapped. "The people of this village consider him to be some sort of god or a warrior-saint like Saint

Michael. He is no god and he surely is not a saint.''

"I never claimed to be anything but a man,'' Clint said. "And I'm no better than any other man here.''

"Then I can do anything you can, *gringo*,'' Raul insisted. "And I demand an opportunity to prove myself to you and to all the people of San José who think you are such a great, grand, glorious hero.''

"You don't have to prove anything to anyone, Raul,'' Clint assured him. "Especially not to me.''

"You will not call me by my Christian name, Adams,'' the young man snapped. "Address me as Medoza. *Comprende?*''

"Okay, Medoza. I don't expect you to be friendly, but I don't see why you should be stupid either. You've never been in a gunfight, have you? Veaga here is a former *federale* so he'll be able to handle himself when we catch up with Gila. You won't be anything but a burden to us. To put it bluntly, Medoza, you aren't qualified for the job.''

"You're wrong, Adams,'' Raul answered. "Have you ever tried to read sign on hard ground or after a sand storm? It can be very difficult to track in the desert. Too difficult for a tired old *gringo* gunfighter and an overaged *federale*.''

"Overaged?'' Veaga growled. The big man was perhaps thirty-five years old, but his hair and beard were already laced with gray. "You think I'm a feeble old man, *chico?*''

Veaga stomped over to a shed which contained a simple forge and some fundamental blacksmith tools. He found a horseshoe and carried it back to the crowd. The ex-*federale* glared at Raul and clenched the curved iron in both hands.

"Watch this,'' Veaga snarled.

He tugged the horseshoe, pulling each end in a fist. His face contorted into a mask of exertion as he pulled harder. The crowd gasped as they watched Veaga pull the horseshoe into a straight bar.

"You still think I'm too old, *chico*?" he demanded, tossing the metal at Raul's feet.

"You're not a tracker, Veaga," Raul replied simply. "I am."

Clint Adams shrugged. "So you say. But every tracker I've ever met who was worth a damn was quite a bit older than you, fella."

"I've been reading sign since I was five," Raul insisted. "I'm the best you'll find in San José."

"Uh-huh," the Gunsmith muttered. "Father Rameriz, do you know if this guy's telling the truth or not?"

"Raul is an excellent tracker," the priest answered.

"Well, I guess you'll be useful after all, Medoza," Clint admitted.

"My son," Rameriz began, "I think you should reconsider."

"I'm not a very good tracker," Clint confessed. "We might need Medoza."

"I wish to speak with you, my son," the priest told Clint. "Come with me, *por favor*."

Father Rameriz turned and marched back to his church. The blind man's cane tapped its way up the risers to the top step. The Gunsmith followed.

"Have you gone mad?" Rameriz demanded.

"A lot of folks think so," Clint answered.

"Surely you realize Raul hates you for what happened last night. Yet you want to allow this man to ride with you after the *bandidos*?"

"He's a tracker."

"You didn't seem to think you needed one before," the priest remarked.

"I didn't know there was one available."

"The bandits have not been trying to cover their tracks so far," Rameriz insisted. "You've had no trouble following them without Raul's help."

"He still might prove useful."

"He may have volunteered simply because he hopes to get a chance to kill you out there."

"Or he might be trying to regain his *machismo* after what happened last night," Clint suggested.

"Or both," the priest mused. "He can come back a hero even if he comes back alone."

"You think he'd murder Veaga too?" Clint asked.

"Raul feels he's lost his honor as well as his wife," Rameriz said. "He knows his wife came willingly to your bed last night. Then you thrashed him as well. That may indeed drive him to commit murder."

"Well," the Gunsmith sighed. "You might be right, but I sort of feel I owe Raul an opportunity to prove himself and reclaim his *machismo*."

"You did not know Elena was married," Rameriz insisted. "You did not shame Raul on purpose."

"That's beside the point as far as Raul is concerned," Clint said. "I still want to give him that chance."

"Are you certain you haven't got another reason, my son?" the priest asked.

"What do you mean?" the Gunsmith raised his eyebrows.

"If Raul dies or you're forced to kill him, then you could claim Elena yourself."

"I don't want Elena," Clint assured him. "All I really want right now is to get my horse and gun back. My second big wish is to take care of Gila and that little sneak Stark Collins."

"And you're willing to risk traveling with a vengeful husband like Raul Medoza to accomplish this?"

"I'd make a partnership with the Devil himself if it would help me to take care of business."

"I hope you are not making such a deal without realizing it, my son." The priest sighed. "Souls are vulnerable to damnation. Take care to protect yours, Clint."

"You concentrate on souls," the Gunsmith told him. "That's your job, Father. But I've got my own job to do."

FIFTEEN

The Gunsmith tugged on the mule's rope bridle. The animal stubbornly protested. Clint pulled harder. The mule brayed and tried to bite Clint. The Gunsmith dodged the snapping teeth and lightly punched the beast on the snout.

"Goddamn jackass bastard," the Gunsmith muttered as he yanked the reins. "We're just gonna get some rest, you dumb son of a bitch."

"You must like horses better than mules," Julio Veaga remarked with an amused chuckle.

"I like just about anything better than *this* mule," Clint growled.

"Mules are usually smarter than horses," the ex-*federale* remarked.

"You don't know Duke," the Gunsmith told him as he strained to tow the mule into an improvised corral consisting of several ropes strung between two cottonwood trees and a pair of boulders.

"Duke?" Veaga wrinkled his brow. "That is the name of the big black horse you rode when you fought el Espectro, no?"

"That's him," Clint confirmed. "The best partner a fella ever had and I'm going to make those bastards pay in blood for kidnapping him."

"Kidnapping him?" Veaga smiled. "You think of this horse as a person, no?"

"Yeah," the Gunsmith admitted. "And I don't care if that sounds crazy to you or not."

"I was a horseman in the *federales*," the big Mexican said proudly. "I know how attached a man can be to his mount. Still, I like mules too. They are strong and able to do more heavy work in the desert than a horse."

"And they're as uncooperative as hell," Clint complained.

"That's because they're smart and stubborn." Veaga grinned. "Like us, no?"

"I hope we're as smart as we are stubborn," the Gunsmith muttered as he shoved the mule's rump to get it to enter the corral.

Veaga tied two ropes across the gap to seal the corral. The other two mules were already inside. The trio had traveled several miles into el Barriga del Diablo. They decided to set up camp when twilight fell. The men put together the corral and removed canteens, leather pouches of food and other supplies from the backs of the mules.

Clint and Veaga watched Raul gather wood for a fire. The big man curled his lip and growled like a surly dog. The Gunsmith smiled.

"Easy, Julio," he urged. "Don't bite him unless he does something to deserve it."

"He's still breathing, isn't he?" Veaga sneered. "That is enough."

"Did you always have such a friendly attitude toward *Señor* Medoza?"

"I never thought much of him one way or the other until today," Veaga answered.

"Has he been a good husband to Elena?" Clint asked, trying to make the question sound as casual as possible.

"I don't know," Veaga admitted. "I was more concerned with starting my own family than I was with how other men handled theirs. Then my wife died during childbirth and I lost interest in just about everything for a while."

"I'm sorry, Julio," the Gunsmith said. "There's nothing worse than losing someone you love."

"Have you ever been married?" the big Mexican asked.

"No," Clint replied. "But I've still lost people I cared about. People I loved."

"It is different when your wife dies," Veaga told him. "I not only lost the woman I loved, I buried all hope for a new life when I put her body and the stillborn infant's into the ground. Dreams about family, about raising children and watching them grow to adulthood . . . all were gone forever."

"That must be about as much pain as a man can endure without dying or going crazy," Clint said with genuine sympathy.

"I wanted to die," Veaga admitted. "And maybe I did go a little *loco* for a while. To be honest, San José doesn't really mean much to me now. I don't know why I stayed on after Maria died. Guess I didn't have anywhere else to go."

"Why did you volunteer for this?" the Gunsmith asked.

"Why not?" Veaga shrugged. "I don't have anything to lose except my life and I don't care too much about that."

"I do," Clint commented. "I don't want any of us to get killed. Especially me."

The big Mexican roared with laughter. He swatted Clint on the shoulder so hard the blow almost knocked the Gunsmith off balance.

"I like an honest man, *amigo*," Veaga declared. "And don't worry. I hate *bandidos* enough to want to see them pay for their vicious crimes. This gives me something to live for, no?"

"I'm so glad," Clint nodded, rubbing his sore shoulder.

"Raul is the one you'll have to worry about," the ex-*federale* warned. "There is a touch of *loco* in that one. He's trying to prove his *machismo*. That can make a man very bold and very careless."

"I know," the Gunsmith agreed. "But he's done okay so far."

"No one has started shooting at us yet," Veaga commented. "This isn't going to end without bloodshed, Clint."

"I wouldn't think that would bother you, Julio," Clint commented.

"Oh, it does not bother me at all," Veaga smiled. "You're the one who wants to live."

"Working with you guys is sure going to be a different kind of experience," the Gunsmith muttered, shaking his head with dismay.

After a simple meal of tacos and beans, the trio sat

by the campfire and sipped coffee from blue tin cups. Raul had remained silent most of the trip. He hadn't spoken a dozen words since they'd left San José.

"We'd better post guards tonight," Clint advised.

"You think Gila suspects someone might be following him?" Veaga asked.

"I'm not worried about the *bandidos*," Clint replied.

"So you think I might try to slit your throat while you sleep, Adams?" Raul chuckled coldly. "The idea is appealing, but I promise to resist the temptation."

"If I was worried about that," the Gunsmith began, "I'd tie you up before I'd close my eyes around you. Sorry to disappoint you, Medoza, but I'm more concerned about Yaqui Indians sneaking into our camp and slitting our throats than I am about you. I had a run-in with three of them yesterday and I'd just as soon not have another one."

"Yaqui." Veaga frowned. "I had almost forgotten about those *indio* devils. You're right, Clint. We should post a guard. Who gets the first shift?"

"Medoza does," Clint answered.

"Why?" Raul demanded.

"Because there's a greater chance the Yaqui will strike later tonight. You're less experienced at this sort of thing than Julio or I, so you get first shift. Besides, I don't trust you as much as I trust Julio."

"You'll take the first shift, *chico*," Veaga said, "or I'll break both your legs."

"Just relax," Clint urged. "*Both* of you. We've got enough to worry about with Gila and the Yaqui out there."

"At least the Yaqui are made of flesh and blood," Veaga mused. "Not iron."

"Jesus," the Gunsmith muttered. "You don't really believe that breastplate makes Gila invulnerable to bullets?"

"I saw Juan shoot Gila," Veaga declared. "The bullet hit him in the chest. The armor protected that *bandido* demon, Clint. You'd better believe it because it is the truth."

"What sort of gun did this fella use?" Clint asked, still finding the story difficult to accept.

"An old cap and ball pistol," the former *federale* answered.

"Thirty-six caliber or a forty-four?" the Gunsmith wanted to know.

Veaga shrugged. "I'm not sure."

"Well, my guess is the gun was a smaller caliber Navy or Police Colt," Clint stated. "Juan probably loaded the chambers with a small amount of black powder. The lead ball was too small to knock Gila on his ass and it didn't have enough charge behind it to penetrate that armor plate."

"Perhaps you're right," Veaga replied. "But you might not be so sure of yourself if you had seen that incident for yourself, *amigo*."

"I've come up against some mighty rough fellas," Clint stated. "But I've never seen a man yet who couldn't be stopped by a well-placed forty-five slug."

"Then Gila may prove to be a new experience for you, Clint," Veaga told him simply.

The Gunsmith took the final guard shift from three in the morning until daybreak. He patrolled the camp and kept all senses tuned to detect danger. Clint walked around the area slowly, his right hand resting on the walnut grips of the Remington revolver holstered on his hip.

He glanced at the two blanket-clad figures sleeping on the ground. Clint kept a watchful eye on Raul Medoza. Although he had tried to seem nonchalant about Elena's jealous husband, Clint was highly suspicious of Raul.

Clint had realized it was risky to bring Raul on the mission; he wasn't certain why he'd done so. Had he felt obliged to give Raul a chance to recover his *machismo*? Did he hope to somehow compensate for the wrong he'd unwittingly done to Raul? Perhaps he'd get a chance to save the young farmer's life. But would this truly redeem him in Raul's eyes?

Or was it possible Father Rameriz had been correct? Did the Gunsmith subconsciously want Raul to die? Clint had once felt a great deal for Elena, but he didn't think he had ever loved her. Could he have secretly concealed such an emotion from himself?

A glimpse of movement caught Clint's attention. He dragged the Remington pistol from leather and trained it on the small, pale figure which approached from the shadows.

"Clint?" a familiar voice called softly. "Is that you?"

"Elena?" the Gunsmith stared at the girl as she hurried forward. "For crissake, what are you doing here?"

"Where else should I be?" Elena replied simply.

"Frankly," Clint Adams said dryly, "right now I wish you were just about any place else."

SIXTEEN

Elena Medoza tried to embrace Clint. He caught her arms gently, yet firmly, to stop her. The Gunsmith jerked his head toward the sleeping figure of Raul Medoza.

"Aren't you forgetting about your husband?" he asked stiffly.

"I don't forget," the girl replied, looking up at Clint's stern face. "But I was never able to forget you either."

The Gunsmith shook his head. "You've got a husband, Elena. You shouldn't have made those wedding vows unless you intended to keep them."

"A woman gets lonely when she does not have a man," Elena stated. "I waited for almost two years for you to return."

"I didn't promise I'd come back," Clint told her. "I never promised you anything."

"I know," the girl admitted. "But Raul did. He offered me love, security and commitment. I had thought that was what I wanted from a man. Then you came back into my life."

"I came to find Gila," Clint corrected. "I'm sorry, Elena. I don't love you and I didn't come back to San José to be with you."

"So you have not thought of me over the last two years?" Elena asked sadly.

"I've thought of you from time to time," the Gunsmith admitted. "But I haven't been pining away since we parted."

The girl sighed. "I didn't think you had been. But I hoped you'd still care."

"I do care," Clint assured her. "But I don't care enough."

"That's how I feel about Raul," she declared. "I don't care enough about him."

"Then you shouldn't have married him."

"I already told you my reasons."

"And you got what you wanted." The Gunsmith shrugged. "I'm not going to change. I'll never be able to give you security and commitment because those aren't things I want for myself."

"Or love?" Elena raised her eyebrows.

"Like I already said"—Clint sighed—"Not enough and not the kind you need."

"Are you going to send me back to San José?" Elena inquired, looking down at the ground.

"That would be too dangerous," the Gunsmith explained. "You're lucky the Yaqui didn't attack you on your way here. Try to get some sleep. We'll talk when the sun comes up."

* * *

Raul Medoza was not pleased to find his wife sleeping in Clint Adams's bedroll when he awoke at dawn. The farmer scrambled from his blanket and grabbed Elena to abruptly pull her to her feet. Raul snarled something in Spanish. Clint didn't understand the words, but he could guess their meaning.

Raul shook his wife angrily and drew back a hand to strike her. Clint stepped forward and caught Raul's arm before he could carry out the stroke.

"That's enough," the Gunsmith told him.

The farmer whirled a left cross at Clint's face. The Gunsmith weaved his head out of the path of the fist. Raul staggered off balance slightly and Clint rammed an upper-cut under the young man's ribcage. Raul fell to his knees and gasped painfully.

"Calm down, you idiot," Clint snapped. "Elena didn't come here to fool around with me. She wants to help us fight Gila."

"A woman will just get in the way," Julio Veaga complained. "Get her out of here, Clint."

"Elena fought el Espectro and his *bandidos* in the past," the Gunsmith stated. "She killed several of the bastards. She also saved my life once by bashing in a fella's skull with a rock. Trust me, Julio. This lady is tougher than she looks."

"She must be," Veaga agreed, "in order to walk out here by herself."

"My wife doesn't belong here," Raul declared as he climbed to his feet, massaging his ribcage with one hand. "She should be back at San José, looking after our home."

"Then you take her back, Medoza," Clint told him. "She can't go back alone, not with the Yaqui in the area."

"It would be too dangerous for her to go back alone," Veaga added.

"You can go with them too, Julio," Clint said. "But I still have a score to settle with Gila. I'm not about to let that son of a bitch get away. To say nothing of that little shit Collins."

"You want to be a big hero, Adams?" Raul spat. "Want to impress us with your *machismo*, eh? You can not shame me, *gringo*."

"I don't want to shame you," Clint growled. "I don't give a shit what you think anymore. I've tried to consider your feelings, but you've been such a snotty asshole, I don't really care anymore."

"I'm staying too," Elena insisted. She canted a Henry carbine over her shoulder. "And none of you can make me go."

"I'm your husband!" Raul snapped. "You took a vow before God to obey me. Now, I order you—"

"To do what?" she demanded. "To leave with you? Are you afraid to face Gila?"

"Damn you, bitch," Raul hissed. "We'll stay with Adams and fight the *bandidos*."

"Your decision, Medoza." Clint sighed. "Make up your mind once and for all."

"You heard my decision, *gringo*," Raul hissed. "And when this is over, I'll settle with you as well, Adams."

"I can hardly wait," the Gunsmith said dryly.

They continued to follow the bandits' tracks. The desert sun gradually grew hotter, but they had plenty of water with them. Elena had brought three more canteens as well as some extra food and the Henry repeater. She took turns riding on the men's mules. Each man walked for a couple hours to reduce the strain on their animals.

By noon, they had covered several miles in the formidable wasteland known as the Devil's Belly. Except for the plentiful hoofprints and an occasional cigarette or cheroot butt, they found no sign of the bandit gang.

Until they spotted smoke in the distance. The thick column of gray billows suggested a fire larger than a campfire. Clint dismounted from his mule and drew the Remington revolver to check its cylinders to be certain they were not clogged by grit.

"How do we handle this, Clint?" Veaga asked, checking his own Winchester.

"I'll go ahead and scout the area," the Gunsmith replied. "The rest of you stay here with the mules."

"I will go with you," Raul announced, climbing down from his mount and drawing his own Colt pistol.

"No," Veaga said. "I'm better qualified to be a scout."

"You're also better qualified to take command if I get myself killed, Julio," Clint stated. "Stay here with Elena. If you hear any shooting, better head for cover and keep out of sight while you wait to see if anybody comes looking for you."

"All right," the big man agreed reluctantly. "But you be careful, *amigo*."

"Okay, Medoza," Clint told the young farmer. "Just remember this is a scouting mission, not an assault. We want to keep out of sight. We only want to get a good look at the enemy's camp. We don't want a fight. Understand?"

"I am not stupid," Raul complained. "Of course I understand."

"Good," the Gunsmith said. "Because if you foul up I'm going to break your goddamn neck. Let's go."

Clint and Raul walked toward the smoke. There was little cover available to conceal them, but the pair made the most of the sagebrush and boulders in the area. Clint was surprised to discover Raul handled the task well. The younger man moved quietly and kept low as he scrambled from one shelter to the next.

"The smoke smells like roasting meat," Raul whispered when he joined Clint behind a boulder. "The *bandidos* must have decided to barbecue a pig or something."

"Something," the Gunsmith replied grimly. "I hope you've got a strong stomach, Medoza."

Raul was puzzled by Clint's remark until they drew closer to the charred remnants of a small farmhouse. Little more than an adobe hut, the inside of the dwelling had been set aflame. The doorway was scorched and the reed roof had burned until it fell in.

A charred corpse was sprawled across the threshold. Clint wasn't certain which sex the deceased had been. Clothing, flesh and muscle were all but gone. Only tattered bits of cloth and blackened skin remained. Muscles had been burned to the bone.

"*Madre de Dios,*" Raul gasped in horror. "This is what we smelled. Why did the *bandidos* do this?"

"The bastards probably stopped here and demanded food and supplies," Clint replied. "The farmer refused or tried to resist so they punished him for his attitude. Nice guys, huh?"

"Do you think that"—Raul gestured at the burned

corpse—"do you think it was dead before they torched the house?"

"I hope so," the Gunsmith stated. "But I don't really feel like getting a closer look at that body to see if it has any bullet holes which might answer your question."

"Neither do I," the young Mexican confessed. "And I don't want Elena to see this either."

"No need for her to," Clint agreed. "But we'd better tell her about this—in detail. I want her to know what kind of people we're dealing with. Maybe she'll decide to go back to San José after all."

"She won't," Raul declared.

"I know," Clint sighed. "Wishful thinking on my part. Elena doesn't scare easy. In fact she hardly scares at all."

"*Sí*." Raul nodded. "But Gila and his *bastardos* are demons straight from hell."

"Yeah," the Gunsmith remarked. "And it'll be a pleasure to send them back where they belong."

SEVENTEEN

As dusk began to claim the sky, the Gunsmith and his group spotted smoke again. This time it was only a faint whisp of gray in the distance. Clint Adams guessed it was from a campfire, perhaps a quarter of a mile away.

"The *bandidos* would probably set up camp about now," Julio Veaga remarked. "I think we've finally caught up with them, *amigo*."

"Let's find out," the Gunsmith said as he dismounted. "Medoza? Want to make another recon trip?"

"Let's go," Raul replied with a nod.

The pair headed toward the smoke. Once again, they made the most of available cover to conceal their progress. The shadows of twilight provided additional camouflage.

Soon they saw the flickering yellow blaze of a campfire. The Gunsmith and Raul continued to advance. They heard numerous male voices, talking, laughing and singing. The pair crept to the cover of a large rock a couple hundred yards from the camp.

They peered into an encampment where a large number of men surrounded a campfire. The group wore bandoliers, sombreros and weapons on their belts. Clint gazed from one dirty, bearded face to the next, searching for someone who fit the description of Gila.

He didn't find the bandit leader in the group. However, he did recognize a face in the crowd. The round, soft features of Stark Collins were partially concealed by the brim of a sombrero, but the Gunsmith easily identified the young bounty killer. Collins was seated on the ground, sharing a bottle of tequila with three *bandidos*.

Two sentries, armed with Winchester rifles, patrolled the perimeter of the camp. Clint made a mental note of their positions. He also noticed something about the bandits' defenses which surprised and alarmed the Gunsmith. Gila's men had a Gatling gun set up.

Clint continued to scan the area. He located a corral which contained more than twenty horses. The Gunsmith's heart raced when he recognized the great black Arabian which stood immobile with ropes tied to his neck to hold the animal still.

Duke, the Gunsmith thought, *if they've harmed you, I'll kill every one of those bastards.*

Raul tugged on Clint's sleeve. The Gunsmith turned to see what the farmer wanted. Raul pointed at an odd pair within the camp, who seemed totally out of place with the rest of the gang.

One was a tall man with a thick midsection and a balding dome. He wore a tan uniform which had been smeared with greasy food and dirt. The buttons and shoulder boards had been torn away. The man's face was bruised and one eye had swollen shut.

A woman sat beside the soldier. She was tall and slender with the fine features of a classic beauty. Her long raven black hair hung loosely about her shoulders. The front of her blue lace dress was ripped open to expose large, perfectly shaped breasts.

Both the soldier and the woman sat with their backs against a boulder. Their ankles were bound by ropes and their hands were behind their backs, the wrists no doubt tied together as well.

A *bandido* was stationed near the prisoners. The sentry glanced about, apparently concerned that his comrades might be watching. Then he knelt beside the woman and grabbed one of her breasts. He fondled her roughly. The woman spat at him. The *bandido* cursed and swatted the back of his hand across her lovely mouth.

The soldier shouted something. Clint couldn't hear what the guy said, but whatever it was didn't please the sentry. The guard quickly rose and angrily lashed a boot into the male prisoner's face. The soldier slumped against the girl. Blood oozed from split skin at his cheekbone.

Two *bandidos* immediately rushed forward and seized the sentry. The guard opened his mouth to protest, but one of his comrades rammed a knee into his groin before he could speak. The man convulsed in agony as the two enforcers dragged him away.

The Gunsmith had seen enough. He tapped Raul on

the shoulder and jerked his head toward where Elena
and Julio waited. The farmer nodded. Clint and Raul
silently slipped away into the night.

"Who do you think those prisoners are?" Julio
Veaga asked after the Gunsmith told what he'd seen at
the bandit camp.

"I can only guess," Clint answered. "The guy in
the uniform is either a *federale* or a *rurale*. Must be an
officer who they hope to sell back to the military."

"And the woman?" Elena inquired.

"Probably plan to ransom her too," the Gunsmith
replied. "The other bandits sure got pissed off when
the guard roughed up the prisoners, so I figure they
want to keep those two healthy. Gila must feel those
hostages can gain him a handsome profit."

"There must be at least twenty *bandidos* in that
camp," Raul stated. "I don't know how the four of us
are going to take a force that size."

"Worse," Veaga added. "They've got a Gatling
gun. Where did a bunch of *bandidos* get their hands on
a thing like that?"

"Maybe that little farmhouse was more than it appeared to be," Clint mused. "But that doesn't matter
now. We've got to come up with a plan."

"How do four people fight twenty?" Raul demanded.

"Especially when they've got a Gatling gun as
well," Veaga commented.

"The Gatling might just work in our favor," the
Gunsmith remarked.

"Do you have an idea, Clint?" Elena inquired.

"Yeah," he replied. "But I don't know how well
you folks will like it."

"I'm sure we won't like it," Veaga said. "But unless somebody else can come up with a better idea, we'll do it."

"You haven't heard my plan yet," the Gunsmith warned.

EIGHTEEN

The plan was simple. They'd wait a few hours to give the *bandidos* time to either fall asleep or get drunk. Of course, there would still be sentries on duty. The Gunsmith and Julio Veaga would have to dispatch the guards as quietly as possible.

Elena and Raul would wait beyond the perimeter of the camp. They would cover Clint and Veaga in case anything went wrong. After the sentries were out of the way, Clint planned to get to the Gatling gun and turn it on the *bandidos*.

If all went well, Gila's gang would surrender when they found themselves staring into the muzzles of the big, rapid-fire weapon. Otherwise, the Gunsmith and his team would have a hell of a fight on their hands. The Gatling wouldn't really give them an advantage. Clint knew that the multibarreled firearm tended to jam after a few rounds were fired from it. He hoped the *bandidos* weren't aware of this quirk.

Despite its flaws, the Gunsmith's plan seemed the most logical choice of action under the circumstances. All the risks were considered and everyone agreed to accept them. Thus, Clint Adams and his allies crept through the darkness to the enemy camp once more.

Hours crawled by as they waited for the majority of the bandits to go to sleep. Many had already passed out from consumption of tequila. Others, however, seemed determined to chat away until dawn. An eternity seemed to pass before some of these *bandido* windbags finally crawled into their bedrolls.

Only the three sentries were still up and about. The guard stationed by the prisoners wasn't the same man who had been dragged away by the two *bandidos* after he'd assaulted the captives. The new sentry did not molest the prisoners, no doubt fearful that he would suffer whatever fate his comrade had endured.

Clint was glad the two perimeter guards had elected to patrol their area in a regular pattern. This was a common mistake by inexperienced and poorly supervised sentries. Hopefully, this meant they'd be relatively easy to ambush. However, trying to overpower a man quietly is never easy.

The Gunsmith had never favored knives as weapons and he wasn't certain he could handle a knife properly to take out a sentry. Instead, Clint selected a thick cottonwood branch for a club. Julio Veaga didn't like knives either. He chose to use a weapon which he was quite familiar with—his bare hands.

The ex-*federale* jumped one of the guards before Clint was in position to handle the second sentry. Veaga simply grabbed the *bandido* from behind and gripped his jawbone with one hand. His other hand seized the man's hair. Veaga twisted the guy's head and broke his neck as easily as one might a pencil.

The second sentry heard the ugly crunch of bone and turned to see Veaga drag the first guard into the shadows. The *bandido* gasped and raised his Winchester. He was about to brace the buttstock against a shoulder when the Gunsmith rushed forward and swung his improvised club at the man's skull.

The guard turned abruptly, startled by Clint's attack. The club missed the bandit's head and struck the sentry's forearm, knocking the rifle from his grasp. Clint quickly rammed the end of his club into his opponent's solar plexus.

The sentry gasped and doubled up. Clint raised the cudgel and prepared to strike the bandit in the skull, but the guard suddenly lunged for his fallen Winchester.

The Gunsmith threw himself onto the man's back. Both men fell and Clint remained on his opponent's back as the sentry landed face first in the dust. The Gunsmith quickly slid the club under the bandit's jaw and grabbed each end of the stick in his fists.

Clint planted a knee at the small of the guard's spine and pulled with all his might, breaking the man's back.

"Luis?" the third guard, stationed by the prisoners, called out softly.

He advanced slowly, rifle held ready. The bandit had obviously heard the sounds of a struggle and suspected something might be wrong. The Gunsmith quickly gathered up the sombrero and rifle from the man he'd just killed. He donned the hat and staggered forward, using the Winchester for a crutch.

"Luis?" the sentry asked, confused by the figure which stumbled toward him.

"*Sí*," the Gunsmith replied, straining his voice to

disguise it and to conceal his accented Spanish. *"No se preocupe, amigo."*

"¿Qué?" the guard said as he drew closer, wondering what was wrong with his comrade.

Clint suddenly whirled and whipped the stock of the Winchester across the bandit's face. The man collapsed to the ground and the Gunsmith stamped the butt of the rifle behind the guard's ear to be certain he wouldn't get up for a while.

The Gunsmith headed for the Gatling gun, walking past a dozen bandits who lay sleeping on the ground. Clint glanced at the captives. The soldier was either asleep or unconscious, but the woman stared at the Gunsmith. Her wide, sensuous mouth fell open in astonishment as she watched him move to the Gatling.

"Shit," Clint hissed under his breath.

The Gatling wasn't loaded.

"Cristo!" an angry voice snarled.

A bandit rose from his bedroll and pointed a pistol at the Gunsmith. Clint ducked behind the Gatling and braced the Winchester against his hip. Pistol and rifle roared in unison. The *bandido's* bullet rang sourly when it ricocheted off the steel frame of the Gatling gun. Clint's shot, however, did not miss its mark. A .44 slug sheared off the top of the bandit's head.

"Oh, shit," the Gunsmith groaned as he watched more bandits spring up from their blankets, hands clawing for weapons. "So much for doing this the easy way."

NINETEEN

Gunshots erupted from all directions. Clint Adams dropped to the ground and lay prone behind the Gatling gun. Bullets whined against metal and spat up dirt near the Gunsmith, but none of the projectiles struck flesh.

Clint fired back, choosing his targets as the bandits dashed for cover. He blasted a Winchester round through an enemy's ribcage as the man ran for the shelter of a boulder. Another *bandido* whirled and aimed his rifle at Clint's position, but the Gunsmith was faster. He pumped a .44 slug through the hollow of the man's throat before the Mexican outlaw could trigger his weapon.

Elena, Raul and Veaga also opened fire on the *bandidos*. The enemy fell, their bodies torn by bullets. Yet plenty of Gila's killers survived and returned fire ruthlessly. A salvo of bullets pelted the positions of the

Gunsmith and his allies beyond the perimeter.

Clint fired two hasty rounds at the bandits and rolled to a new shelter behind a cottonwood tree. Bullets splintered bark from the trunk. The Gunsmith aimed the Winchester along the side of the tree and drilled a slug through a *bandido*'s heart.

He worked the lever action to the rifle. The spent cartridge casing popped out of the breech. Clint trained the Winchester on another bandit and squeezed the trigger. A feeble click told the Gunsmith the weapon was empty.

Clint discarded the Winchester and drew the Remington revolver. He saw two *bandidos* convulse as bullets crashed into them, fired by Elena and Raul. Another Mexican butcher prepared to fire back at them. The Gunsmith aimed the Remington carefully and triggered the pistol. A bullet slammed into the side of the enemy gunman's head.

The Gunsmith glanced over his shoulder to see two *bandidos* about to attack him from the rear. Clint rolled over on his back and rapidly fired two shots at the assassins. One man dropped his pistol and clasped both hands to his bullet-shattered face. He wilted to the ground—dead.

The other assailant screamed when a bullet burned a destructive path through his biceps. The man's arm recoiled from the impact and his revolver flew from his open fingers.

But he kept coming. The son of a bitch charged forward and swung a kick at the Gunsmith. Clint was taken off guard by the man's boldness. The boot struck his hand and sent the Remington hurtling from his grasp.

The Gunsmith braced his shoulders against the ground and lashed out a kick of his own. Clint's foot caught the *bandido* squarely in the balls. The man doubled up with a high-pitched whine. Clint rocketed up from the ground fist first. He hit the bandit with a hard right cross which knocked his opponent out cold.

Clint turned to retrieve his pistol. A boot stamped on the Remington and pinned it to the ground. Stark Collins pointed a Smith & Wesson revolver at the Gunsmith's face and thumbed back the hammer.

"Well, well." The young bounty hunter smiled. "Fancy meeting you again, Mr. Adams. I thought I killed you a couple days ago."

"Maybe I'm a ghost," Clint said dryly.

"Then you won't mind if I shoot your face off," Collins sneered. "Now raise your hands, Adams. Unless you want me to test your ghost story."

"Can't you take a joke, kid?" the Gunsmith asked as he raised his hands.

"Sure I can." Collins shrugged. "But you killed a lot of Gila's men tonight. I don't think he'll find that very funny."

Clint sighed. "Maybe I should show him some card tricks."

The shooting ceased abruptly. Julio Veaga suddenly stumbled into view. Three *bandidos* clung to the big man like a trio of savage wolves trying to bring down a grizzly bear.

Veaga snarled and rammed an elbow into an opponent's midsection. The guy folded with a gasp and Veaga slammed a fist into another bandit's face. The punch knocked the outlaw seven feet. The third *bandido* swung a fist into Veaga's stomach.

The ex-*federale* smiled and grabbed the bandit by the ammunition belts which crisscrossed his chest. Veaga lifted his opponent off the ground and whirled about to hurl the man like a sack of potatoes. The hapless *bandido* crashed into two of his brothers in blood, knocking them to the ground.

Veaga pivoted, fists held ready to take on more opponents. However, he found himself staring into the muzzles of half a dozen guns. Reluctantly, the big man raised his hands in surrender.

"Looks like your side lost, Adams," Stark Collins remarked with a chuckle.

The Gunsmith did not bother to reply. His full attention was locked on the lifeless figure two *bandidos* carried into the camp. Gila's henchmen dumped the body on the ground as if it was a bag of garbage.

"Christ, Adams," Collins muttered when he noticed the corpse. "Why did you bring a woman out here? I know you must have had trouble finding somebody stupid enough to join you on your suicide crusade, but did you have to bring a woman?"

"Just shut up," Clint said stiffly, staring at Elena's corpse.

Her breasts were covered with blood. Her unblinking eyes gazed up into the night sky. The girl's face, however, seemed peaceful and lovely in death.

"You'd better not act high and mighty here, Adams," Collins warned. "Gila is already pissed enough at you. Don't make things worse."

"You're concerned about me, kid?" Clint snickered.

"I've got nothing personal against you, Adams. This is just business with me. Gila and his boys might see things different. They do things you've never imagined in your worst nightmares. Bear that in mind when you meet the boss.''

TWENTY

The Gunsmith finally met Gila face to face. It was an unnerving experience. The *bandido* leader seemed to be a creature from another world, a cold, hard world of blood and metal.

Gila slowly approached Clint Adams. The bandit chief was less than six feet tall, yet his physical presence was awesome. His limbs were thick with coils of muscle and his head was large with a beetle brow beneath a mop of curly black hair. Gila was like a giant that had been compressed into a more compact frame.

His broad face was stern with a wide, hard mouth. Several jagged scars ran across his features and a misshapen nose divided small, piercing black eyes. His appearance really was reptilian.

Although Clint had heard about Gila's armor, he wasn't prepared for what he saw. It was not an old brass Spanish breastplate. Gila's armor was made of iron and it covered his torso like a turtle's shell. Clint guessed the armor was more than an inch thick.

The Gunsmith saw this with his own eyes, yet he could hardly believe any man could actually live inside such a heavy case of iron. How could Gila bear the additional strain in this brutal climate?

Clint glanced down at the metal gauntlets on Gila's hands and forearms. Steel spikes, each two inches long, jutted from the gauntlets from knuckle to elbow. Gila smiled coldly and nodded at the Gunsmith.

"You're Clint Adams?" the bandit leader inquired. "The one they call the Gunsmith?"

"Some folks call me that." Clint nodded.

"I was almost sorry when Stark told me he'd killed you during that fight back at the pass," Gila remarked. "I've heard so much about you, it was a pity to only get to see your corpse. But it seems you've risen from the dead like Lazarus. That means we have something in common. I too am reborn after a violent and treacherous death."

"We spirits have to stick together," the Gunsmith replied dryly.

"I'm afraid you're going back to the hereafter," Gila told him. "And this time we'll make certain you stay dead."

"Gonna drive a stake through my heart?" Clint asked.

"Something like that," the *bandido* stated simply. "Death can come in many forms, *señor*. Fast or slow. Painless or filled with agony."

"I don't think I'm in a position to try to deal with you, Gila," the Gunsmith commented.

"No, you are not," Gila agreed. "You were lucky, Adams. You shouldn't have tried that luck by coming after me after our first encounter. Are the Texas Rangers really offering enough money for you to die for them?''

''Money isn't the reason I accepted the job, Gila—or whatever your real name is,'' Clint said.

''I am Gila,'' the bandit chief declared. ''Who I was in the past hardly matters now.''

''That's right.'' The Gunsmith nodded. ''Whatever happened to you in the past doesn't justify your actions. Nothing can excuse the way you've butchered innocent people.''

''Innocent?'' Gila laughed. ''You do not know what your Texas ranchers are like, Adams. Of course, you're a *gringo* so Texans treat you differently than they do a Mexican.''

''You haven't been treating some Mexicans very well either, Gila,'' Clint remarked.

''I have never killed one of my countrymen unless he forced my hand,'' Gila replied.

''We passed a small farmhouse where you'd brought your odd version of sunshine and cheer,'' the Gunsmith commented. ''You remember that farmhouse, or was that too long ago?''

''Didn't you notice there were no livestock or even chickens at that farm?'' Gila inquired. ''It had been abandoned long ago. There were no farmers or *peónes* living there.''

''But there were some *federales*?'' Clint asked.

''*Rurales*,'' Gila corrected. ''But how did you guess?''

''You guys had to pick up that Gatling gun somewhere between San José and here,'' Clint replied. ''To say nothing of those two prisoners you've got tied up over there.''

''Let me introduce you.'' Gila turned to the captives. "The young lady is Louisa Alverez. Her father is Don Carlos Alverez, one of the wealthiest ranchers in Sonora."

"And you're holding her for ransom. What about the soldier?"

"Captain Santos of the Sonora *rurales*," Gila answered. "We're hoping his fort commander will care enough to pay for the captain's return."

"Kidnapping can be more risky than plundering Anglo ranches, Gila," the Gunsmith told him. "The Mexican government might not care what happens to some Texans north of the border, but they might feel differently about kidnapping their important citizens. Important citizens have money and friends in high places."

"Not that high," the bandit stated. "Besides, we hadn't intended to kidnap these two. We happened to come across the *rurale* patrol which was escorting *Señorita* Alverez back to the Don's ranch. The patrol had stopped at that old farmhouse for a rest. When the *rurales* saw us, they started shooting. We were forced to defend ourselves."

"And Louisa and Santos just happened to be the only survivors, and you decided to try to make a profit with them."

"The opportunity presented itself." Gila shrugged. "We tossed the dead soldiers into the house and set fire to it. Then we took the lady, the captain and the Gatling gun with us. Unfortunately, the latter seems to have suffered from our last gun battle."

"Yeah," Clint said dryly. "A lot of bullets meant for me hit the Gatling instead."

"The gun has been ruined," Gila sighed. "But we

still have our hostages . . . and you, Adams.''

"And what are you going to do with Julio and me?"
the Gunsmith asked. "Bear in mind, this assault was
my idea. I'm responsible. Julio isn't to blame so you
can't punish him the same as me."

"Nobody twisted my arm to ride with you, Clint,"
Veaga declared stubbornly. "Let this iron-plated toad
have his fun. I will not kneel before a twisted freak
such as he."

"You two and the unfortunate girl who was killed in
the battle," Gila began, "killed nine of my men and
wounded three others. You can not be allowed to live
after this. I'm just trying to decide whether I should let
my men torture you both to death or grant you the
consideration of a quick and relatively painless
death."

"Tell me something, Gila," the Gunsmith said.
"You speak fluent English and you seem to be an
intelligent man, even if you are crazy. Why are you
leading a bunch of ragtag *bandidos?* What pleasure do
you find in murdering innocent people and destroying
Texas ranches?"

"Let me tell you a story about a certain Texas
ranch," Gila hissed through clenched teeth. "It was
owned by a cattleman. Everyone believed he was a
good man. He went to church on Sunday, never beat
his wife or mistreated his children. The men who
worked for him also believed he was a good man, a fair
man. Even the young Mexican blacksmith who worked
on that ranch, respected *Señor* Dobbs.

"Then," Gila continued, "one night one of the
cowboys claimed he'd been robbed. The other cowboys decided the greaser blacksmith must have done it.

So eight of them confronted the young Mexican and held him at gunpoint. They demanded that he return the stolen money. The blacksmith was not the thief, but they did not believe him when he claimed to be innocent.

"So the cowboys tried to beat a confession out of the blacksmith," Gila declared. "They hit him with their fists and gun butts. They knocked him down and kicked him in the ribs, in the face and in his *cajones*. The blacksmith still did not confess to a crime he had not committed. But the cowboys were not convinced. They tied the greaser to a rope and fastened the other end to the saddlehorn of a horse. Then they took turns dragging the blacksmith. They laughed as they rode the horse across the prairie."

Gila glared at the Gunsmith. "Have you ever been dragged in such a manner, Adams? Your body is bounced and thrown against the earth. Your skin is scraped off like old paint and your bones crack and crunch as they break."

The bandit chief gazed down at the ground. "The cowboys left the blacksmith more dead than alive. Left him for the vultures and the coyotes. However, an old Mexican hermit found the young man and carried him to his shack in a cart.

"The old man treated the blacksmith's injuries as best he could, but several of the bones in the young man's ribcage did not knit properly. Together, they made a sort of leather harness to protect the blacksmith's damaged torso. The young man slowly grew stronger and recovered from his ordeal as well as he ever would. He stayed with the hermit and helped the old man who was growing weak with age. Two years later, the hermit died."

Gila smiled bitterly. "At last the blacksmith got up enough courage to return to the ranch," he said. "The young man was a broken, sickly wreck, but he was able to walk with the assistance of crutches. He met with *Señor* Dobbs and told him what had happened. Dobbs heard his story and simply shrugged. He told the young man there was nothing he could do. The rancher had hired another blacksmith and the Mexican was too sickly to work anyway. *Señor* Dobbs, kind and generous *Señor* Dobbs, gave the young man twenty dollars and sent him away.

"The young blacksmith died soon after that," Gila stated. "He became a different person. The change took time, of course. Progress was slow, but the crippled and scarred young Mexican had no friends or family. Only a desire for justice. Revenge, if you like. He added plates of armor to his harness. He used light sheets of metal at first and gradually used heavier plates as his body grew stronger. Muscles developed and eventually he adapted to a shell of iron."

Gila tapped his metal chest. "And thus a new being was born. Gila was created—strong, determined and invulnerable. This powerful new being found followers by appealing to the most honest of man's emotions—greed. Gila and his army returned to Alan Dobbs's ranch and avenged the young blacksmith who had died so long ago."

"I can't condone that," Clint said, "but I can understand why you attacked Dobbs's spread. Still, why did you continue to raid other ranches after you got your revenge?"

"Because men like Dobbs are corrupt and evil," Gila answered. "They have acquired wealth and power by trampling on others. They smugly play God as they rule over their subjects like lords. Their arrogance has condemned them. They have victimized others so it is proper that they now become victims themselves.''

''I've met lunatics like you before,'' the Gunsmith declared. ''Bitter people who want the whole world to suffer because they've suffered injustice from a handful of people. Your breed makes me sick to my stomach, Gila. You're so full of self-pity and hatred you don't have any room left in your heart for any other human emotion.''

''How unfortunate,'' Gila replied mildly, ''for *you.*''

TWENTY-ONE

Louisa's unexpected scream startled the Gunsmith. He turned to see two *bandidos* dragging the girl to a horse blanket on the ground. The pair were busy ripping her clothes off as Louisa struggled hopelessly against their combined strength.

Clint Adams reacted by instinct. He forgot that a dozen guns were aimed at him as he bolted over to the rapists. Clint heard a voice shout something in Spanish. He ignored it and closed in behind the nearest attacker.

The Gunsmith clasped his hands together and swung them to chop the *bandido* in the nape of the neck. The first rapist groaned and fell unconscious against the girl. His partner glanced up with alarm to see Clint's boot rocketing toward his face. The heel crashed into his mouth, cracking bone and shattering teeth.

"Freeze, Adams!" Stark Collins ordered, thrusting the muzzle of his S&W against the Gunsmith's right temple. "Try another stunt like that and I'll blow your brains out."

Louisa stared up at him, her eyes open wide with surprise. Clint hadn't seen her up close until now. The girl was indeed beautiful. Her large dark eyes expressed gratitude for Clint's action and admiration for his courage.

"Listen, Adams," Collins snapped, "you've got enough problems of your own. Don't worry about this gal. Whatever these fellas want to do to her, they're gonna do it. Gettin' yourself killed isn't gonna stop them."

The Gunsmith slowly rose and helped the girl to her feet.

"Hey, Gila," he began, "I thought you didn't want your boys to mistreat the hostage. If your men hurt her, this lady could die. Better tell them to keep their pants on before they screw you right out of a ransom."

"So rape is a violation of your principles, eh?" Gila remarked with amusement. "And you want to force your standards on the rest of us. Your arrogance is incredible, Adams. What would you be like if you were not an unarmed prisoner?"

Actually, the Gunsmith was not unarmed. His .22 New Line Colt hideout gun was still concealed under his shirt. However, Clint didn't see how the diminutive pistol could help under the circumstances. There were too many opponents and all of them were armed with weapons far more deadly than his little .22.

Still, as long as he was alive there was hope. If the bandits got careless he might be able to draw the New Line and possibly train it on Gila to try to get the bandit chief to order his men to drop their weapons.

No, the Gunsmith thought. Gila would not surrender. The crazy bastard really believed his armor made him bulletproof. Even if Gila ordered the others to lay down their guns, it was unlikely they'd do so.

Yet, there was one possibility of salvation. The *bandidos* had brought in Elena's corpse, but they hadn't found Raul Medoza. If the young farmer had escaped alive, he might launch a one-man assault on the *bandidos*. A good distraction could give Clint a chance to use the tiny Colt or to get his hands on a better firearm.

However, the Gunsmith realized this wasn't very likely. If Raul had escaped, he was probably either wounded or too frightened to try to help. The farmer wasn't apt to be coming to Clint's rescue. That meant the Gunsmith could only cling to one last hope.

If Clint Adams had to die, he didn't intend to go to the grave alone. The Gunsmith wasn't afraid of death, but he didn't relish the idea of being skinned alive or burned to death over a campfire with a pole stuck up his ass. If he didn't have any choice left, Clint would draw his New Line Colt and shoot as many bandits as he could before the others gunned him down.

"*You're* not in charge here, Adams," Gila declared. "I am. Don't ever give orders in my camp, *gringo*. You take them. *Comprende?*"

TWENTY-TWO

"Cobardes!" Julio Veaga shouted. *"Hijos del putas!"*

Clint Adams recognized the words for "cowards" and "sons of whores." So did the *bandidos*. Veaga spat out a string of rude Spanish which was beyond Clint's limited command of the language.

"Your friend wants to fight, Adams," Gila translated. "He's challenged any three of my men to take him on in hand to hand combat."

"I want you, toad," Veaga snarled. "If you can find two men who think they have enough guts to attack somebody who doesn't wear skirts, I'll take all three of you on at once."

"Shit, Julio," the Gunsmith groaned. "Have you lost your mind?"

"No, Clint," Veaga smiled. "They're going to kill me anyway, so what have I got to lose?"

"Very well, *chico*," Gila laughed. "I'll fight you.

Just me, stupid one. I don't need any help to handle an oaf like you. Say your prayers one last time before you die.''

The bandit leader ordered his men to stay back. Veaga nodded at Gila and stepped forward. Clint Adams steered Louisa away from the combatants.

"Your friend must be mad," she remarked.

"Maybe," the Gunsmith agreed. "But I saw him break a fella's neck as if it was a dry twig."

"He doesn't have a chance," Louisa sighed. "And neither do we."

"We're not dead yet, lady."

He hoped the fight between Gila and Veaga would distract the other bandits long enough to allow him to draw his New Line Colt.

Stark Collins held a familiar weapon in his fist. Clint immediately recognized the modified double-action Colt which Collins pointed at his chest.

"Plan to shoot me with my own gun, kid?" Clint inquired.

"It'd be sort of ironic if that happened," Collins mused. "I've kept this gun hidden in my saddlebags because the others might try to steal this fancy Colt if they knew I had it."

"Hope you've been taking good care of my gun," the Gunsmith stated. "I want it back in good condition."

"What for?" Collins shrugged. "Want'a be buried with it? You just relax and watch the fight. I'll just stay here and keep an eye on you just in case you try to pull some sort of trick."

Gila unbuckled his gunbelt and handed it to another

bandido as he approached Julio Veaga. The pair squared off. The former *federale* was about six inches taller than the bandit boss, but it was difficult to say which man was more muscular. However, Gila's armor and spike-studded gauntlets gave him an obvious advantage.

Clint guessed that Veaga's probable strategy was to get behind his opponent and apply a lethal neck hold. The idea might work if Veaga were fast enough. Clint hoped the bandit's armor would slow him down enough to allow Veaga's plan to succeed.

Veaga moved forward, his fists held ready for combat. Gila raised his arms and waited for the larger man to make the first attack. Veaga obliged. He closed in fast and faked a right cross. Then he threw a quick left at Gila's face.

The bandit lifted his right arm. Veaga cursed when his forearm struck the gauntlet. Spikes ripped his sleeve and tore flesh beneath it. Veaga retreated and lashed a kick to Gila's midsection. His boot bounced off iron. The bandit's only reaction was an expression of mild amusement.

The ex-*federale* faked another right and swung his left. Gila again moved to block it, but Veaga's second punch was also a feint. He swiftly darted behind his adversary. Gila tried to dodge, but he was too slow. Veaga attacked the bandit from the rear.

Clint Adams held his breath as he watched Veaga seize the *bandido* leader's head with both hands and prepare to snap his neck with a hard twist. Gila's arms suddenly rose and raked steel spikes across Veaga's hands and wrists. The big man howled with pain and anger. He released Gila and stumbled backward, blood dripping from his torn flesh.

Gila pivoted and lashed a spiked forearm at Veaga. Again, the armor slowed him down. Veaga dodged the attacking limb and nailed Gila on the jaw with a solid punch. The blow would have rendered most men unconscious, but Gila's head barely moved from the impact of Veaga's fist.

The *bandido* executed an overhead attack with a gauntlet-clad forearm. Veaga instinctively blocked the stroke with his own. Sharp blades pierced Veaga's flesh once more. The big man gasped and Gila followed up with a vicious punch to Veaga's face.

Veaga fell to the ground. Blood oozed from a gashed cheek. Loose skin flapped at the corner of his mouth. But Veaga wasn't out of action yet. He scooped up a fist full of sand and hurled it at Gila's face.

''*Cabron!*'' the bandit rasped when dirt flew into his nostrils and eyes.

Clint's hopes soared when Veaga scrambled to his feet and swung a powerful right cross to his opponent's face. This time Gila's head bounced backward from the punch. Veaga lashed out with his other fist.

He screamed when Gila's gauntlets snared his arm like the jaws of a vicious steel trap. Blood splurted from a severed artery and crimson splashed Gila's breastplate.

The *bandido* leader rammed a fist into Veaga's stomach. The ex-*federale* doubled up with a choking gasp. Gila's left arm snaked out and wrapped around his opponent's neck to apply a simple head lock. Then he slammed his right forearm down on the top of Veaga's skull.

Gila released his opponent. Julio Veaga collapsed in

a twitching heap. Blood-dyed streaks of red in his hair and a pool of crimson formed around his torn throat. Gila blinked his eyes to clear them as he gazed down at his vanquished foe. The other *bandidos* cheered their leader's victory.

"Your friend was very good, Adams," Gila admitted, speaking thickly with a split lip. "But not good enough."

"He would have taken you if you hadn't been wearing those goddamn spikes on your arms," the Gunsmith snarled.

"Perhaps," Gila allowed as he unstrapped one of the gauntlets. "But that's beside the point now, isn't it?"

"Go to hell, you bastard," Clint spat, angered by the death of his friend.

"You'll be going there before I will, Adams," Gila remarked. He stripped off the gauntlet to use a bare hand to wipe his eyes and bloodied mouth.

"*Jefe.*" Collins addressed Gila as chief. "I'd like to ask for permission to kill Adams. I've followed his career for years and I've never had a chance to kill a gunfighter with a reputation like his."

"You had your chance, Stark," Gila replied, strapping the gauntlet back on his arm. "The rest of my men want to avenge the death of their comrades. They will be allowed to kill Clint Adams. And they'll have all the time they need to make his death as painful as possible."

TWENTY-THREE

Stark Collins lowered the modified Colt revolver and sighed with genuine disappointment.

"Sorry, Adams," he said. "I tried."

"You expect me to thank you?" the Gunsmith scoffed.

"Hell, I would have killed you quick," the bounty hunter explained. "A nice quick bullet to the head—"

Then Stark Collins's skull exploded. His brains splashed out of the shattered bone like gray chili from a broken clay bowl. The report of a rifle echoed from beyond the perimeter of the camp.

"*Que la chigada!*" a voice cried.

"You said it, fella," Clint Adams remarked as he watched the bandidos scramble for cover.

More gunshots roared from outside the bandit base. Two more members of Gila's terror troops were cut down before they could flee. Several *bandidos* returned fire, aiming at the muzzle flash of their unseen opponents' weapons.

Clint pulled Louisa to the ground and plucked his double-action .45 from the lifeless hand of Stark Collins. With the modified Colt pistol in his fist, the Gunsmith felt whole once again.

"Stay down," he told Louisa. "And don't get up until the shooting is over."

Two *bandidos* turned their attention—and their weapons—to the Gunsmith. Clint reacted faster than a cornered cougar. His Colt snarled two shots so fast they sounded like one. Both bandits staggered backward with a bloodied bullet hole in the center of their chests.

The Gunsmith charged forward and followed a group of bandits who fled to the corral. Several of the outlaws had already saddled their mounts and prepared to flee the area. A shaggy *bandido* with a gold tooth was about to climb onto the back of his horse when he spied Clint Adams.

"Gringo bastardo!" the bandit hissed as he aimed a revolver at the Gunsmith.

Clint's pistol spat fire and a slug punched through the man's upper lip. Three teeth, including the gold one, popped out of his mouth as the bullet drilled upward to pierce bone and penetrate the *bandido*'s brain.

A volley of gunshots exploded from the members of Gila's gang who had already mounted their horses. The Gunsmith threw himself to the ground and rolled to the cover of a cottonwood tree which was part of the improvised corral.

The shooting from the perimeter of the camp continued. Clint heard men scream, but he wasn't certain if the voices belonged to *bandidos* or the mysterious gunmen beyond the camp.

Clint saw the shadowy figures of mounted bandits bolt into the darkness. He aimed carefully and fired a .45 round into the back of one of the fleeing horsemen. The Gunsmith felt no shame in shooting the bandit in the back, well aware of the type of men who belonged to Gila's gang.

However, the horseman did not tumble from his saddle. Clint noticed that the rider was thickly built and muscular. He wondered if the man was Gila himself. Whoever the *bandido* may have been, he and several others galloped into the night and vanished.

TWENTY-FOUR

"Rurales!" a voice shouted from the darkness. *"Sus manos arriba!"*

Within the camp, only two *bandidos* were still alive to obey this order. They stepped into the open and raised their hands to show they had no weapons.

Five figures approached the camp. They were dressed in white cotton shirts, trousers and straw sombreros. However, the rifles they carried and the gunbelts strapped around their waists revealed they were not *peónes*.

"Clint Adams!" one of the men shouted. "Are you all right, *Señor* Adams?"

"I'm fine," the Gunsmith replied. "Thanks to you gents. *Gracias, amigos.*"

"Uno momento," one of the bandits began. "You speak English and you're dressed like *peónes*. If you really are *rurales*, where are your badges?"

"Badges?" a rifleman sneered. "Badges? We don't need no stupid badges."

To prove his point, the man stepped forward and quickly swung his rifle to butt-stroke the *bandido* across the mouth. The outlaw fell with a groan.

"Louisa?" Clint called.

"I am here," the woman answered as she rose unsteadily, holding her dress together as best she could.

"*Señorita* Alverez," a rescuer addressed her with a formal bow. "*Yo soy teniente Rodriguez, señorita. Donde esta el capitan?*"

"*Alli esta, teniente,*" Louisa replied, pointing at the battered figure of Captain Santos who still sat against the boulder, bound and helpless.

The Gunsmith turned his attention to Duke, hobbled in the corral. The big black gelding recognized Clint immediately. Duke neighed a cheerful greeting and bobbed his head as well as the restraining ropes allowed.

"Don't fret, big fella," Clint assured his horse. "I'm coming."

He climbed into the corral and quickly freed Duke. The Arabian gratefully rubbed his snout against the Gunsmith's chest. Clint patted Duke and hugged his neck.

"It's okay, fella," Clint told Duke. "We've both been through a lot, but we're back together again now."

The gelding raised and lowered its head as if to agree.

"*Señor* Adams?" a tall lean man spoke as he approached the corral. "I am Lieutenant Rodriguez. It is an honor to meet you, *señor.*"

"I'm damn glad to meet you too," the Gunsmith answered as he led Duke from the corral. "How'd you fellas happen by here?"

"We were suppose to join Captain Santos and the escort team for *Señorita* Alverez at a deserted farmhouse several kilometers from here," the lieutenant explained. "When we arrived, we found only death and destruction. We suspected Gila and his gang may have done this. No other *bandido* gang is large enough to do such a thing."

"Why are you dressed like *peónes*?" Clint asked. "To disguise yourselves so the bandits wouldn't recognize you from a distance?"

"Sí, señor," Rodriguez confirmed. "If the *bastardos* realized a squad of *rurales* were following their trail they would have tried to ambush us or at least cover their tracks to try to lose us."

"I'm surprised you fellas were able to read sign in the dark," the Gunsmith remarked. "Whoever does the tracking for your squad must be part bloodhound."

"Not at all," Rodriguez replied. "Your friend *Señor* Medoza found us. We had set up camp a couple kilometers from here and he happened to find us. Medoza explained how you and his wife and the big *hombre* tracked Gila from San José. He told us how you attacked this camp, but the *bandidos* had killed *Señora* Medoza and captured you and the big one. He alone had managed to escape."

"So Raul led you here?" Clint asked.

"Sí." The *rurale* captain nodded. "Do you wish to see him?"

"Yeah," the Gunsmith answered.

Raul Medoza knelt by the lifeless body of his slain

wife. He cradled Elena's head in his lap as he sobbed and uttered whispered words which Clint could not understand. Yet he needed no translator. Grief is a universal language.

The young farmer glanced up at Clint, tears streaming down his cheeks. The Gunsmith realized words were useless. He nodded at Raul, then turned to leave him to grieve the death of his wife in private.

Lieutenant Rodriguez and another *rurale* helped Captain Santos climb onto the back of a horse. The senior officer's arms and legs had been bound so long the circulation of blood to his limbs had been cut off. Rodriguez turned to Clint Adams.

"We're going to return to Fort Juarez," the lieutenant declared. "I fear our captain has suffered internal injuries from the beatings those scum gave him, and we must also get *Señorita* Alverez to safety."

"I don't see Gila among the dead," Clint stated. "He must have been one of the bandits who managed to escape."

"*Si*," Rodriguez agreed. "And we'll hunt the pig down later. Several of my men were killed in the battle. With only a handful of *rurales*, we are not able to pursue Gila's *bandidos*. Besides we have *el capitan* and the lady to consider."

"I understand," the Gunsmith assured him. "But I'm not going to give that son of a bitch enough time to get away."

"You should come with us to the fort, *señor*."

"I'm going after Gila as soon as I can find my saddle and gunbelt," Clint insisted. "He's got too much blood on his hands. The blood of people I cared about. He's going to pay for that."

"Reconsider, *señor*," the lieutenant urged. "You do not know how many of his men ride with him. The odds are surely in Gila's favor—"

"Good luck, Lieutenant," the Gunsmith said.

"*Sí, señor*," Rodriguez sighed. "Go with God."

The Gunsmith turned to Louisa. The girl gazed up at him sadly with her beautiful dark eyes. She shook her head slightly and managed a weak smile.

"I don't suppose you'll change your mind and agree to come with us," the girl remarked hopelessly.

"This is something I have to take care of personally," Clint replied. "And I have to do it now."

"Killing Gila won't bring your friends back to life," Louisa told him. "Neither will getting yourself killed."

"Gila has to be stopped," the Gunsmith stated simply. "And I've got a few personal reasons to want to put him out of business myself."

"*Machismo*." She spat out the word. "Is that all you men ever think of? All of you are always trying to prove how brave you are or you're running off to fight in wars or kill someone for revenge."

"Revenge is part of my reason for wanting to see to Gila in person," Clint admitted. "As long as he's alive and running around free, he'll continue to hurt and kill innocent people. Besides, I was hired to do a job and I've got an obligation to finish it."

"Of course," Louisa sighed. "Honor is important to a man like you. Yet, it is sad that honorable men seldom live to become old."

"I plan to be around for a few more years, Louisa," Clint assured her. "And I hope to see you again before I head back for Texas."

"I pray that will happen." She smiled.

"That makes two of us," the Gunsmith said with a grin.

TWENTY-FIVE

Clint Adams found his saddle, gunbelt and Springfield carbine among the bandits' gear. He strapped the saddle to Duke's back and slid the Springfield into the boot. Raul Medoza approached, a Winchester canted across his shoulder.

"Where do you think you're going, Adams?" the farmer demanded.

The Gunsmith frowned. Raul might well blame him for Elena's death . . . and Clint wasn't sure if he was at fault or not. His hand dropped to the holstered Colt on his hip.

"I'm sorry about Elena," Clint told him. "I'm sorry for your sake as well as my own."

"You are going after Gila, no?" Raul asked.

"That's right," the Gunsmith confirmed.

"Then I am going with you," Raul announced.

"Gila and his butchers killed my wife, Adams."

"I figure about ten of the bastards rode out of here," Clint remarked. "Five to one odds."

The farmer shrugged. "Better than ten to one."

"Yeah," Clint admitted. "How are you at tracking in the dark?"

"The *bandidos* won't travel very fast or very far in the dark," Raul said. "We'll make slow progress until dawn, but so will they."

"We'll catch them," Clint declared firmly.

"Not by standing around talking about it," Raul replied bluntly.

Tracking by night is difficult for even the best experts in the field. Fortunately, the *bandidos* had left a very visible trail. Raul was able to read sign by moonlight as he and the Gunsmith followed the tracks on foot.

Riding a horse in the dark is extremely risky since both man and animal are unable to see obstacles clearly. Clint and Raul led their mounts by the reins as they walked. They ventured across the desert slowly, traveling yard by yard as patiently as stalking shadows.

They had barely covered the first mile when they discovered the twitching body of a horse, lying on its side. The animal whinnied in pain. As Clint drew closer, he saw that the horse's right foreleg was broken.

Then they noticed another figure sprawled on the ground several yards from the injured horse. It was the corpse of a *bandido*. His guns, ammunition belts and boots were gone; a large rock near his head was smeared with crimson.

"The horse must have tripped," Raul remarked. "Probably stepped in a prairie-dog hole in the dark."

"And the bandit was thrown off when the animal stumbled," Clint added. "Fella must have been riding his horse at full gallop. He was hurled more than ten feet."

"The rest of the gang learned from his mistake," Raul declared. "There are bootprints leading away from here. I believe the *bandidos* are now on foot, leading their horses as we have been doing."

"And there's one less son of a bitch in the pack," the Gunsmith commented, glancing down at the dead man. "Sure wish I could shoot that horse. Hate to let it suffer, but a gunshot would probably be heard by the bandits."

"I'll take care of the animal," Raul announced.

He drew a bowie knife from a belt sheath and approached the injured horse. Raul straddled the poor beast and sunk the seven-inch steel blade between the animal's eyes. The horse died instantly.

"Jesus," the Gunsmith rasped. "I'm sure glad *you* did that. I don't think I could have."

"I thought the great Clint Adams could do anything," Raul remarked dryly.

"Hell," Clint muttered. "I realize I wronged you although I didn't do it on purpose. Still, I've tried to make up for it. Maybe I can't compensate for what I did, but can't you give me a little credit for trying? We're both on the same side. Can't you just concentrate on hating the *bandidos* for now?"

"I do not hate you, Clint Adams," the farmer replied. "When Elena used to speak of you, I resented the affection and respect she felt for you. But, I also admired you after hearing so many stories about your courage.''

''Stories get exaggerated.''

''I don't think that has happened in your case, Clint,'' Raul said. ''I was jealous of you and angry when I found you with Elena. Yet I must admit you are a better man than I am.''

''Bullshit,'' Clint snorted. ''I'm a drifter with a knack for getting into trouble. Nothing so great about that. You saved my life when you brought the *rurales* to rescue us.''

''I encountered the *rurales* by accident,'' the young farmer confessed. ''I was frightened, Clint. When the shooting started, I froze. Everyone else fought back, but I was too scared to move. Then Elena was shot. She fell dead beside me. I saw the *bandidos* capture you. Instead of staying to help, I ran.''

''That turned out to be the best thing you could have done,'' Clint stated. ''You found the *rurales* and brought them back to the camp to attack the bandits.''

''But I ran in fear, Clint,'' Raul admitted. ''I am a coward. I was afraid.''

''Who isn't afraid, Raul?'' the Gunsmith inquired. ''If you don't know fear, you can't appreciate its opposite. Courage isn't acting without fear. It doesn't take any guts to do something you're not afraid of. Courage is tackling what you fear.''

''Then I must be braver than I thought,'' Raul said with a nervous laugh.

Clint shrugged. ''Everyone is. Whenever somebody faces something he or she fears, that is courage. Whether you face an opponent with a gun or one inside yourself, it is still courage.''

"Perhaps the opponent within is a greater threat," Raul mused.

"It always is," the Gunsmith confirmed. "But Gila won't be a pushover either."

TWENTY-SIX

The Gunsmith and Raul Medoza mounted their horses after the dawn sun rose to illuminate the sky. They continued to follow the bandits' trail until it led them out of the Devil's Belly.

"Where the hell are they heading?" Clint muttered. "Guatemala?"

"There are a few small farms in this area," Raul said. "Farther south there are some towns. Hard to say where Gila and his scum are heading."

"They're probably not sure themselves," the Gunsmith mused. "Gila's band have been driven off their regular turf. Now they're probably just looking for some place to lay low for a while."

"Their tracks are still clear enough," Raul said. "It's difficult to segregate hoofprints when there are so many tracks which have overlapped, but I'd say there are at least eight horses. Perhaps nine."

"That's about what we figured. We'll have to take

extra care from now on. If the bandits see us coming we'll lose the element of surprise. Two against nine in open combat is lousy odds.''

"*Sí,*" Raul agreed. "Too lousy."

Three hours later, they spotted a farm in the distance. The bandit's trail seemed to extend directly to the place. A herd of sheep grazed on the grassy meadows beyond a simple adobe house and a weather-beaten barn. Three horses were tied to a hitching rail in front of the farmhouse.

"Do you think the *bandidos* are down there?" Raul whispered to the Gunsmith.

"That barn could contain nine men and horses," Clint answered. "But why are three tied to the rail?"

"Maybe Gila and his top lieutenants decided to use the house as sort of an officers' billets," the farmer suggested.

"Could be," Clint agreed. "We'd better approach the barn from the blind side. That should keep anyone inside the house from seeing us through a window as well.''

"If we have to fight any bandits in the barn the gunshots will alert the men in the house.''

"Yeah, but it's more likely we'll find a large number of bandits in the barn than in the house. I'd rather attack the larger group and take a chance of being jumped by the smaller than the other way around.''

"*Sí,*" Raul nodded. "Let's do it now, Clint. I don't want to have much time to think about this.''

Raul ground-hobbled his horse. Clint didn't worry about Duke wandering off. He drew his Springfield from its boot. Raul followed Clint's example and unsheathed his Winchester.

They cautiously circled the farm and crept toward its blind side, then stealthily moved to the side of the barn.

Clint held up a hand to urge Raul to stay put while he slipped around the corner. The Gunsmith braced the Springfield against his hip and thumbed back the hammer as he moved to the open door of the barn.

He took a deep breath, held it and thrust the gun barrel along the edge of the doorway. Clint stared inside. The barn appeared to be empty.

A bullet smashed into the wooden framework of the barn door. Clint dove across the threshold and shoulder-rolled across the straw-laced floor. He hopped to his feet, the Springfield held ready.

Another slug splintered the doorway. The Gunsmith saw the flame of a gun muzzle jet from one of the windows of the house. The door to the house burst open. A figure wearing a sombrero appeared and pointed a pistol at the barn.

"Gringo cabron!" the bandit snarled as he fired his handgun.

The third bullet also struck wood. Clint Adams raised the carbine to his shoulder and waited. A rifle barrel jutted from the window. Clint fired his Springfield. The face behind the rifle vanished and the bandit's weapon slipped over the sill to clatter on the ground.

"One down," the Gunsmith muttered as he worked the lever action of his carbine to jack another cartridge into the breech.

The *bandido* in the doorway fanned the hammer of his revolver and blasted two rounds into the barn. Clint remained behind his cover; however, the report of a rifle cracked from the corner of the barn.

A scream of agony burst from the bandit as he stumbled across the threshold with a bloodied hole in his chest. Clint glanced toward the edge of the barn to see Raul Medoza fire his Winchester again. The young farmer pumped a second round into the *bandido*'s upper torso.

"Die, *bastardo*!" Raul exclaimed with delight as he watched the bandit topple to the ground.

"Raul!" Clint shouted. "Get back!"

But he was too late. A gunshot roared from the house and Raul Medoza's head recoiled violently. He dropped his Winchester and collapsed with a soft moan.

The Gunsmith saw the third *bandido* silhouetted in the doorway. As the killer swung his rifle toward Clint's position the Gunsmith triggered his Springfield. A howl of pain followed and the *bandido* fell against the door frame. A crimson stain dyed his shirt above his belt buckle.

The outlaw tried to brace his rifle on a hip to fire back at the Gunsmith. Clint beat him to the trigger and blasted the bandit's skull to bits with a well-placed .45 slug.

Clint stayed behind his shelter and waited to be certain the last opponent inside the house was dead. The Gunsmith saw no more movement within the dwelling. He cautiously approached, still holding the Springfield ready.

The two bandits on the ground were as dead as a pair of rusty coffin nails. Clint noticed one man's arm was in a sling and the other had a crude bandage on his thigh. Apparently, both had been wounded back at the bandit camp. They must have been unable to keep up the pace set by the rest of the gang. The trio had decided to take their chances at the farm while the others rode on.

Clint entered the house. The interior was neat, with simple furniture and a well-swept wooden floor. He found the third bandit lying dead by the window, his face bathed in blood.

The Gunsmith emerged from the house and walked to the still form of Raul Medoza. He looked down at the corpse and shook his head sadly.

"Shit, Raul," Clint rasped. "Why didn't you stay put?"

He knelt beside Raul's body and placed two fingers on the dead man's eyelids to gently push them shut.

"Never mind, *amigo*," Clint whispered. "I think I know why."

"Drop that gun, mister!" a female voice ordered.

The Gunsmith turned to see the twin barrels of a twelve-gauge shotgun pointed at his chest.

TWENTY-SEVEN

The shotgun was held by a handsome woman clad in a checkered shirt and Levi trousers. Her blond hair was bound in a ponytail. Large firm breasts strained the fabric of her shirt. Clint found her face and figure appealing, but not her stern expression or the shotgun which was still aimed at him.

"I'm not an outlaw, ma'am," the Gunsmith told her.

"Not likely ya'd admit to it if ya be one, laddie," the woman replied with a Scottish accent. "I won't be tellin' ya to drop that gun again."

"Okay," Clint said, lowering the Springfield to the ground. "You live here, lady?"

She nodded. "Aye. I'm Sheena McCabe and I've killed more than one blackguard who tried to take what rightly belonged to me."

"Well, I'm Clint Adams," he explained. "And I just killed the bandits who were playing house on your property. Doesn't that prove I'm not your enemy?''

"It proves ya weren't their friends," Sheena replied. "Could be ya only killed 'em cause ya be wanting the same things they did.''

"Miss McCabe—''

"*Mrs*. McCabe," the woman corrected. "My husband died a while back.''

"I'm sorry," the Gunsmith told her.

"Ya be more than sorry if ya think 'cause I be a widow woman I can't take care of meself," Sheena snapped. "Ya be dead, laddie.''

"Will you relax, lady?" Clint sighed. "And don't point that shotgun at me. It isn't necessary.''

"So ya tell me," she said dryly, but she lowered her weapon. "Now let's hear your story. And it best be a good one.''

The Gunsmith told her about his quest to hunt down Gila. The woman frowned when he described Gila and the bandit gang.

"Aye," she said. "Those blackhearted scum were here. I was in the field, working on my potato garden when the bandits arrived. I hid in the meadow, usin' the sheep for cover. Watched those hoodlums march into me house and barn, lookin' for the owners I suspect. Aye. The man with the chest of iron was among that lot. Not likely I be forgetting that one.''

"He does sort of stand out in a crowd," Clint agreed. "Sorry about shooting so many holes in your house and the barn.''

"Never mind 'bout that," Sheena assured him. "I just be thankful ya took care of those villains. Too bad 'bout your mate. Say his wife was killed by the bandits just last night?''

"That's right," the Gunsmith confirmed.

"Well, at least neither of them will be missin' each other now. Dreadful lonely being a widow."

Clint nodded. "I believe you. I'd better get rid of these bodies for you, ma'am."

"Get the one out of me house first," Sheena said. "I don't care to be fixin' us dinner with a corpse stinkin' up me kitchen."

The Gunsmith buried Raul Medoza a couple of hundred yards away from Sheena McCabe's farm property. The *bandidos* did not merit such consideration. Clint simply draped their corpses over the backs of their own horses and led the animals back to the prairie.

He dumped the three corpses on the ground and crudely covered them with sand and rocks. Clint didn't leave any marker for the bandits' communal grave. The outlaws were buried under a simple pile of loose stones which might or might not keep the vultures and coyotes from dining on them. The Gunsmith didn't really give a damn either way.

Clint returned to the farmhouse, weary and hungry after three hours of manual labor. Sheena had prepared mutton, boiled potatoes and coffee. The Gunsmith was delighted to discover the meal waiting for him on her kitchen table.

"Hope ya like mutton, laddie," Sheena declared.

"Mutton will be fine," he assured her. "But I'd rather be called Clint than laddie, if you don't mind."

"Sorry. I don't mean any offense by it. You can call me by me Christian name too if you please," she said. "No reason for us to stand on ceremonies now."

"Any idea where Gila's gang might have headed after they rode on from here?"

"There be a small town about fifteen miles south of here called Redencion," Sheena answered. "Legend has it some Jesuit missionaries founded the community about a hundred years ago. Thought they'd convert all the Indians. The town is sure a far cry from what those priests had in mind. Redencion doesn't have any *rurales* or *federales* in the area. Nobody in Redencion cares if strangers want to kill each other."

"Not too fussy about who wanders into town, eh?"

"Some of the residents wouldn't care if ya burned the place to the ground. Don't imagine anybody else would care much either."

"Sounds like a great place," Clint muttered.

"Anything else ya want to ask me?"

"Well"—Clint smiled—"I'm sort of curious about why a nice Scottish girl is living out here in the middle of Mexican nowhere."

"How else does a woman ever get in a damn fool mess?" Sheena sighed. "By listenin' to a man, of course. Me husband thought he could come to Mexico and become some sort of sheep-raising czar. Somehow he got the notion that a sheep herder in this country is like a cattle rancher in the United States. Thought he'd made a bleedin' fortune. Silly sod."

"So you traveled here from Scotland and wound up with this farm?" Clint asked.

She nodded. "Aye. And then James had a heart attack and died. That left me stranded here alone on this worthless farm."

"Where would you go if you left?"

"Back to Scotland, I imagine," Sheena replied.

"But there's no way I can go back. A lass needs money to pay for a trip across the ruddy ocean."

"Would a thousand dollars be enough?" Clint inquired.

"A thousand dollars?" She raised her eyebrows. "That would surely be more than enough. But a man never gives away that kind of money without a reason. If that be what you're suggesting, what would your reason be?"

"The Texas Rangers are going to pay me four thousand dollars for bringing in Gila—dead or alive," Clint replied. "You've already helped me so I figure you've earned part of that reward."

"All I told you was which direction the bandits went and which town they're probably headin' for. That's hardly enough to be worth a thousand dollars."

"It is to me," the Gunsmith told her. "I want that son of a bitch so bad I'd kill him now whether the Rangers pay me or not."

"Didn't ya say ya not be a bounty hunter?" she mused.

"I wasn't hired to kill Gila," Clint explained. "But this is a personal matter now."

"But how are ya goin' to pay me this thousand dollars ya be talkin' about?" Sheena asked.

"I could send it to you later," he answered.

"Send it?" The girl rolled her eyes. "The bloody postman doesn't make deliveries out here, ya know."

"Okay," Clint said. "Then you can come to Texas with me."

"I've never been to Texas. It's quite a way from here, isn't it?"

"Not as far as Scotland."

"Aye," Sheena agreed. "True enough. Still, you have to catch up with Gila first."

"I will."

"Maybe I'd best come along and give ya a hand, if that's . . ."

"No way," the Gunsmith said sternly.

"I've got me shotgun."

"Everybody who has helped me fight those bandits has wound up dead," he told her. "You just stay here and wait for me to come back."

Sheena frowned. *"If* you come back."

TWENTY-EIGHT

"I want ya to make love to me, Clint," Sheena announced when they'd finished eating.

The Gunsmith choked on his coffee. "What?"

"Don't be makin' me repeat something like that," Sheena snapped. "A woman gets lonely. If I can't have nothin' else, I want at least a good memory about a nice lookin' lad like yaself. If ya don't want to do it, I'd be grateful if ya'd just leave and ride on without givin' me any excuses."

"I'm in no hurry," Clint said as he rose from his chair. The Gunsmith took Sheena in his arms and pressed his lips to hers. Clint's skillful hands stroked Sheena's back and ribs.

The girl moaned happily as Clint fondled her breasts. Rigid nipples strained against the fabric of her shirt. The Gunsmith began to unbutton the garment, but Sheena caught his wrists.

"In the bedroom," she urged.

They moved into the next room and Clint stripped off her shirt. Sheena's big, beautifully formed breasts bobbed free and naked. He kissed them, gently biting the erect nipples while he unbuttoned the woman's trousers.

Clint slid Sheena's Levis down her thighs and slowly knelt before her. He tenderly kissed the soft, smooth flesh of her thighs, slowly shifting his mouth to the center of her womanhood.

"Oh, Clint," she sighed.

The Gunsmith pressed his face against the tawny triangle of hair. The strong odor of her female musk increased his desire. Clint thrust his tongue into her and slid it to and fro.

"Lord," Sheena gasped. "Let's get to bed."

The Gunsmith quickly stripped off his clothing and joined Sheena on the patchwork quilt. Naked, they explored each other's bodies with fingers and mouths.

Clint moved his lips to Sheena's breasts and sucked the nipples as his hands caressed her thighs. His fingers slipped between her legs and stroked. She purred happily as Clint moved on top of her.

Sheena found his rigid manhood and guided it inside, then hooked her calves around his thighs to pull him closer.

The Gunsmith slowly pumped his hips to work himself deeper. Sheena soon erupted in an uncontrollable spasm as the first orgasm shot through her like an electrical charge. Sheena's fingernails bit into his biceps as she cried out with pleasure. Her body bucked and convulsed like a wild horse as the second orgasm swept through her. Clint thrust faster, harder, until he too reached the limit.

"God, that was lovely," the girl whispered. "Seems like ages since I've done this with a lad."

"You sure haven't lost your touch," Clint assured her.

"I wish you didn't have to go," she sighed.

"But I do. And I'd better leave soon. I want to be in Redencion before sunset."

"There are five of them, ya know," Sheena said.

Clint shrugged. "The odds are lower than they were when I started this job. But I'm not going to underestimate Gila again."

"You can't afford to make any mistakes," Sheena agreed.

"True. Reckon I've used up my quota of luck on this mission. If I make another mistake it'll get me killed for sure."

"I don't want that to happen," she whispered.

"Neither do I," he assured her. "Neither do I."

TWENTY-NINE

Clint Adams didn't have any trouble following the bandits' trail. Fortunately, Gila and his followers still hadn't made any effort to cover their tracks. The Gunsmith followed the gang's hoofprints for several miles.

Then the enemy of trackers, expert or amateur, threatened to prevent him from continuing the quest. Twilight gradually darkened the sky. Clint realized he wouldn't be able to read sign in the dark. He decided to cover as much ground as possible before nightfall and then make camp. The Gunsmith hadn't slept for almost forty-eight hours and he was exhausted. The rest would do him good. . . .

"I'll be a son of a cross-eyed jackass," the Gunsmith remarked when he saw a number of small adobe buildings in the distance. "Looks like we've found the town of Redencion, big fella."

Duke uttered a curt snort as if to express that he was not impressed by this news.

Redencion wasn't much of a town. And Clint was surprised that there wasn't a bell tower or a crucifix on any of the buildings. If Redencion had a church, it didn't advertise this fact.

Clint decided to dismount and walk the rest of the way. He was grateful for the shadows of twilight which would conceal his features from the watchful eyes of any *bandido* lookout who might be on duty, but he didn't want to risk breaking one of Duke's legs by galloping around in the dark.

The place seemed deserted except for the flickering yellow lamplight visible in the windows of one of the buildings.

Above the entrance of this structure was a crudely painted legend which identified the building as a cantina. An unfriendly figure sat in a chair in the doorway. The man wore a sombrero and had ammunition belts strapped across his chest. A Henry carbine lay across his knees.

Clint watched the *bandido* sentry out of the corner of an eye as he strolled to the livery. The guard watched the Gunsmith, but the man did not make a threatening move or shout to alert the rest of Gila's gang.

"The livery is not open for business, *señor*," a voice whispered from the darkness.

Clint was startled by the sudden appearance of a small, scrawny old man who seemed to have materialized from thin air. Dressed in ragged, poorly patched clothing and a battered straw sombrero, the stranger gazed up at the Gunsmith. A toothless smile split his dirty, bearded face.

"Perhaps I can be of assistance, *señor*," the old man declared. "Allow me to introduce myself. I am el Mendigo."

"*Mendigo?*" Clint frowned.

"*Sí.*" The stranger grinned. " 'The beggar.' A man does what he can for a living, no? One should take professional pride in one's occupation."

"I reckon that's true." The Gunsmith shrugged. "But how do you offer to help me, Señor Beggar?"

"I can slip inside the livery through a loose board in the wall," el Mendigo explained. "It is sort of my personal entrance to the place. You see, I sleep inside with the horses. I can open the stables for you. Then we can take your animal inside and you can pay Diego in the morning, no?"

"But I pay you first, right?"

"Only a few coins, *señor*," the old man replied. "As a beggar, it is not up to me to tell you what contribution you see fit to make."

"Thanks for the offer," the Gunsmith remarked. "But I have a feeling the whole town will be awake pretty soon and I'll have a chance to talk to the hostler in person—if I'm still alive."

"Oh, *señor?*" El Mendigo raised his bushy gray eyebrows. "I think we should talk. I may yet be of assistance to you."

"Oh, yeah?" Clint asked suspiciously. He wondered if Gila might have bought the old man's services as an innocent-looking ally.

"Let's move away from the cantina," el Mendigo urged. "That *bandido* at the door will soon become suspicious if we continue to speak together within his sight."

"Won't he become suspicious if we walk away

together?'' Clint inquired.

"Not if I lead you to the local *casa de las putas*," the old man replied slyly.

"The whorehouse?'' the Gunsmith mused as he followed el Mendigo down the street. "I'm surprised *bandidos* haven't already transported all the local harlots to the cantina."

"Oh, they did,'' el Mendigo told him. "But they finished with the girls about an hour ago. All the *putas* are now home, no doubt licking their wounds. The *bandidos* were pretty rough on the poor ladies."

"You seem well informed, *amigo*."

"A beggar lives by his wits, *señor*,'' the old man explained. "So I try to know as much as possible about what goes on in my town."

"Do you happen to know if all the *bandidos* are inside the cantina right now?'' Clint asked.

"*Sí*.'' El Mendigo smiled. "And I know how to get inside the place without going through the front door."

"Another loose board in a wall?'' Clint inquired dryly.

"No. Merely the back door. Unfortunately, it is probably locked. You can break it down, but that will alert Gila and his *cabrons* to danger."

"How do you know about Gila?'' the Gunsmith asked.

"Everyone has heard of that *bastardo*,'' el Mendigo answered. "Who else would be riding with a group of stinking *bandido* scum or choose to wear an iron plate around his chest?"

"And why do you think I'm looking for Gila?"

"You mention shooting, no?"

"No, I did not."

The beggar smiled. "Not directly. But when a man like you talks about making enough noise to wake everyone in town, a man who wears his gun low on his hip like professional *pistolero*, then what else can he refer to? And who did you come to Redencion to shoot? Unless one of the whores gave you the clap and you've hunted her down for revenge, you must be here to kill Gila."

"You're a clever man, *Señor* Mendigo," the Gunsmith remarked. "Maybe too clever."

"An honorable beggar does not work for *bandidos*," the old man declared proudly. "*Bandidos* steal and murder. They are aggressive and wicked. A beggar is neither violent nor treacherous. Would you insult my profession, *señor*?"

"Certainly not," Clint assured him. "But I still want you to stay right next to me until I get the back door to the cantina open. Okay?"

"I would not think of running around to the front of the cantina to alert the *bandidos*," el Mendigo said curtly. "But I would not think of endangering my own life either. That is not proper conduct for a professional beggar and you have no right to demand such risk of me. I am, after all, a specialist."

"Don't worry," the Gunsmith promised. "You'll be safe enough."

"When you kick in that door those *bandidos* will start shooting—"

"I'm not going to kick in the door," Clint told him. "Just take me to it."

"Very well, *señor*." El Mendigo sighed. "I just hope you will consider my cooperation when you pay me for this."

"Your contribution will be generous," the Gunsmith stated. "But I don't have any money with me right now."

"Then how do you intend to pay me?" el Mendigo inquired with a frown.

"I'll have the money for you after I've taken it from the dead *bandidos*."

"I was afraid you'd say something like that," the old man groaned.

THIRTY

El Mendigo escorted the Gunsmith into an alley which led to the rear of the cantina. Clint Adams removed a small leather packet which contained some gunsmith tools. He knelt before the door and opened the kit.

Clint removed a slender cartridge probe and a narrow hacksaw blade from his packet. Carefully, he inserted both tools into the keyhole. He worked them inside the lock until a dull click rewarded his efforts.

The Gunsmith gripped the doorknob and turned it. The door opened a crack. Clint pulled it shut and drew his .45 from leather.

"You'd better go now," he told el Mendigo.

"*Sí*." The old man nodded. "*Vaya con Dios*."

"May God go with you too, *amigo*." Clint smiled. "And thanks for everything."

El Mendigo hurried from the alley. The Gunsmith opened the door and slipped inside the cantina. He found himself in a storage room behind the bar. Clint advanced cautiously, his pistol held ready.

A beefy *bandido*, dressed in a sweat-soaked shirt, threadbare trousers, and ammo belts, leaned against the counter with his back turned to the Gunsmith. Apparently, he had been elected to act as bartender.

Clint crept closer and peered into the barroom beyond. Two *bandidos* were seated at a table, sharing a bottle of tequila. The fourth was still stationed at the front entrance. Gila sat alone, apart from the others. Like the professional he was, the bandit leader had his back to the wall. He seemed solemn and thoughtful as he sipped beer from a clay mug.

The Gunsmith clenched his teeth, held his breath and charged forward. The *bandido* bartender turned awkwardly, startled by the sound of boot leather on the floor behind him.

The man was drunk, but he still recognized Clint Adams and made a clumsy attempt to draw on him. The Gunsmith closed in fast and slashed the barrel of his Colt across the Mexican hootowl's jawbone.

The bartender fell with a groan. The two bandits at the table cursed in Spanish and leaped from their chairs. The first man reached for his holstered weapon. The Gunsmith's Colt spat double-action death.

The second *bandido* was still pawing at his sidearm when Clint's next round hit him in the chest. Left of center, the slug ripped into his heart. The outlaw fell to the floor in a convulsing, dying heap.

"Mierda!" shouted the bandit at the front door.

He turned and aimed his carbine at the Gunsmith. Clint triggered his Colt a third time. The bullet hit the frame of the guard's weapon. The slug ricocheted off metal and struck the *bandido* in the side of the face, gouging out a chunk of his cheekbone. The man screamed and pulled the trigger of his own weapon.

A stray bullet splintered wood from the corner of the bar. The Gunsmith returned fire and shot the bandit in the chest. The slug kicked the outlaw's body backward, through the open door of the cantina. He tumbled outside to die in the dust.

Clint swung his Colt toward the bandit leader. Gila's face stiffened. His eyes widened with surprise, but Clint still saw no fear in the man's expression. The Gunsmith cocked the hammer of his pistol.

"Get up," Clint ordered. "Get up, you ironclad son of a whore!"

"You've already won, Adams," Gila declared as he slowly rose from his chair. "Kill me and finish it."

"I intend to," the Gunsmith admitted. "But I'll give you a fighting chance. Go for you gun, Gila."

The bandit leader stepped from behind the table. He lowered both hands to the buckle of his gunbelt and unfastened it. The belt and holstered revolver fell to the floor.

"Pick it up," Clint told him.

"No." Gila smiled. "You'll have to shoot me in cold blood, Adams."

"You don't think I'll do it?" the Gunsmith asked.

"I don't think you have a taste for murder, Adams," the *bandido* replied as he stepped forward.

"Killing you will be a public service," Clint stated. "Any court worth a fiddler's damn would execute you anyway."

"So shoot," Gila invited as he moved closer.

"Take one more step and I will," the Gunsmith

warned. "Look, Gila. Maybe I wouldn't shoot an unarmed man in cold blood, but you're not unarmed. I've seen what you can do with those spiked gauntlets. Take another step and I'll blow your head off."

"So I'm supposed to just stand here and wait for you to get enough courage to shoot me?"

The Gunsmith sighed. "No. You can pick up a gun and defend yourself or you can keep coming."

"What if I do neither?"

Clint shrugged. "Then I'll count to three and kill you anyway. One . . . two . . ."

The sound of metal scraping leather suddenly commanded the Gunsmith's attention. He turned to see that the *bandido* bartender had recovered from being clipped on the chin by Clint's pistol. The man sat up and dragged his Trantor from its holster.

Clint quickly stepped forward and kicked the bandit in the face. Blood squirted from his nostrils as his nose was crushed under Clint's boot heel. The *bandido* fell unconscious. His Trantor slipped from uncaring fingers beside him.

Gila took advantage of the distraction and charged. The Gunsmith pivoted to see the ironclad bandit chief rush toward him, his deadly spiked arms raised for attack.

Clint hastily fired his Colt. A round struck Gila in the chest. The Gunsmith heard the sour chime of metal striking metal. Gila staggered backward two steps. Then he smiled and kept coming.

"Oh, fuck," Clint rasped as he aimed his Colt at Gila's unprotected head.

The bandit raised his arms higher at the same instant Clint triggered his pistol. Another slug struck metal. A spark erupted along one of Gila's gauntlets. The *bandido* cursed as his arm jerked from the impact of the bullet. However, he lowered his arms and smiled at the Gunsmith.

"That's six rounds, Adams," Gila snarled. "You're finished."

He lunged forward and swung a gauntlet-covered arm at the Gunsmith. Clint dodged the attack. Gila's arm struck the top of the bar. Wood cracked under the force of the powerful blow.

The Gunsmith lashed out with the empty revolver, trying to club Gila's skull with the walnut butt. The bandit blocked the attack with his other forearm. The Colt struck steel spikes instead of Gila's head. Clint's hand popped open and the gun flew out of his grasp.

"Son of a bitch!" the Gunsmith exclaimed as he slammed a solid left hook to Gila's jaw.

The bandit's head barely moved from the punch. Clint followed up with a right cross to the point of his opponent's chin. Gila grunted and stumbled back a step.

The Gunsmith placed both hands on the counter and vaulted over the bar—feet first. His boots crashed into Gila. The *bandido* cried out in anger as the powerful double-kick sent him staggering backward. Clint grabbed the nearest chair and swung it at his adversary as hard as he could.

Gila quickly ducked his head and covered it with his forearms. The chair struck his iron breastplate. The furniture seemed to explode. Wood shattered like glass. Clint still had a broken chunk of the backrest in his fists. The other parts of the chair were scattered about the room.

And Gila was still on his feet, smiling at the Gunsmith.

The bandit fiend swung a mailed fist at Clint's head. The Gunsmith raised the jagged piece of chair still in his hands and managed to parry the deadly punch. He desperately lashed a kick between Gila's legs. His boot struck iron.

"What the hell?" Clint muttered as he leaped away from another spike-studded forearm slash. "How do you take a piss?"

Gila didn't reply. He swung a sudden cross-body stroke at the Gunsmith. Clint gasped with pain when sharp steel points ripped through his left sleeve to claw the flesh from his forearm.

"I'm going to take you apart, Adams," Gila hissed. "Bit by bit."

"Kiss my ass," the Gunsmith snarled as he thrust a heel-kick to Gila's kneecap.

The *bandido* cursed and stumbled off balance. Clint slammed his fist against the side of Gila's head. He clubbed his knuckles behind the man's left ear. Gila still wouldn't go down. Clint wondered if his skull were made of iron too.

With an enraged howl, Gila whirled and swung a forearm across Clint's chest. The Gunsmith leaped away from his formidable opponent. Needles of pain lanced his torso. Blood oozed from Clint's torn shirtfront.

Gila roared like a furious grizzly and attacked yet again. His spike-covered arms were spread to embrace the Gunsmith in a lethal bear hug. Clint suddenly dropped to one knee, ducking under the bandit's gauntlets. He grabbed both of Gila's ankles and pulled with all his might.

The *bandido* crashed to the floor like a statue in an earthquake. Three floor boards cracked under his enormous weight. Gila hissed like a serpent and slammed a boot into Clint's chest. The Gunsmith was propelled backward into the closest wall.

"*Bastardo*," Gila growled as he awkwardly rolled over to all fours.

He crawled to the nearest corpse and yanked the dead man's pistol from its holster, turning to face the Gunsmith. His eyes blazed with hatred and blood trickled from the corner of his mouth as he thumbed back the gun hammer.

Then Clint Adams shot him in the face.

The Gunsmith had drawn his .22 New Line Colt from its hiding place under his shirt while Gila was taking the revolver from his dead comrade. Clint aimed carefully and triggered the diminutive handgun.

A .22 round hit Gila under his left eye. The bullet cracked the orbital bone and Gila's eyeball popped out of the socket. His head recoiled and a shriek of agony burst from the bandit's throat. The revolver fell from his hand.

The Gunsmith stepped closer and fired another bullet into Gila's skull. The projectile punctured the bandit's left temple and burned a deadly path into his brain. Clint shot him a third time to be certain he was dead. The Gunsmith pumped the last .22 missile through the base of his opponent's skull.

"Now it's over," Clint said breathlessly as he leaned against the bar. "You lose, fella."

THIRTY-ONE

The Gunsmith left Redencion shortly after dawn. He rode Duke and led two other horses behind him. A very unhappy *bandido* with a broken jaw crudely wired together was mounted on one animal. His hands were tied behind his back. The rope was looped across his throat. If the bandit tried to struggle, he would choke himself.

The third horse carried a different type of burden. Gila's iron breastplate and one of his gauntlets were tied to the saddle. The armor seemed harmless without its occupant, like a giant turtle shell, preserved as an innocent curio.

Clint had only traveled half the distance back to Sheena McCabe's farm when he encountered a large group of riders dressed in tan uniforms and sombreros with badges pinned to the crowns. Clint easily recognized the horsemen as *rurales*. Lieutenant Rodriguez led the company of soldiers. He galloped forward and greeted the Gunsmith with a crisp salute.

"Ah, *Señor* Adams," the officer began, "it is a pleasure to see you again. Especially since you are still alive."

"I managed to stay that way," Clint replied dryly.

"It seems you have found a friend, no?" The lieutenant referred to the bandit prisoner.

"Not exactly," the Gunsmith stated. "This fella is the last surviving member of Gila's gang. I'd be glad if you gents would take him off my hands."

"Our pleasure, *señor*," Rodriguez assured him. "And what happened to the pig Gila?"

"He's gone to that big junkyard in the sky," Clint answered.

"I do not understand." The lieutenant frowned.

"Gila is dead," the Gunsmith explained. "He's buried back in Redencion. If you want to find his grave to dig him up and check for yourself, just ask for a fella called el Mendigo. He'll be happy to show it to you for a coin or two."

"A beggar?" Rodriguez wrinkled his nose with distaste.

"A beggar with honor." Clint grinned. "I personally recommend him. El Mendigo is worth his weight in handouts."

"I think we can take your word that Gila is dead," Rodriguez shrugged. "Would you care to ride with us back to Fort Juarez, *señor*?"

The Gunsmith nodded. "Sure. If we can stop by a little farmhouse first and get somebody who helped me find Gila."

"Will this person be traveling with you very far?" the lieutenant wanted to know.

"All the way back to Texas," Clint replied.

"Who is this person?" Rodriguez asked.

"A nice lady farmer named Sheena McCabe."

"Oh?" The lieutenant smiled. "I wonder how she and *Señorita* Alverez will get along?"

"Well"—the Gunsmith sighed—"I guess we'll find out."

J. R. ROBERTS
THE GUNSMITH
SERIES

☐ 30928-3	THE GUNSMITH	#1: MACKLIN'S WOMEN	$2.50
☐ 30878-3	THE GUNSMITH	#2: THE CHINESE GUNMEN	$2.50
☐ 30858-9	THE GUNSMITH	#3: THE WOMAN HUNT	$2.25
☐ 30925-9	THE GUNSMITH	#5: THREE GUNS FOR GLORY	$2.50
☐ 30861-9	THE GUNSMITH	#6: LEADTOWN	$2.25
☐ 30862-7	THE GUNSMITH	#7: THE LONGHORN WAR	$2.25
☐ 30901-1	THE GUNSMITH	#8: QUANAH'S REVENGE	$2.50
☐ 30923-2	THE GUNSMITH	#9: HEAVYWEIGHT GUN	$2.50
☐ 30924-0	THE GUNSMITH	#10: NEW ORLEANS FIRE	$2.50
☐ 30931-3	THE GUNSMITH	#11: ONE-HANDED GUN	$2.50
☐ 30926-7	THE GUNSMITH	#12: THE CANADIAN PAYROLL	$2.50
☐ 30927-5	THE GUNSMITH	#13: DRAW TO AN INSIDE DEATH	$2.50
☐ 30922-4	THE GUNSMITH	#14: DEAD MAN'S HAND	$2.50
☐ 30905-4	THE GUNSMITH	#15: BANDIT GOLD	$2.50
☐ 30886-4	THE GUNSMITH	#16: BUCKSKINS AND SIX-GUNS	$2.25
☐ 30907-0	THE GUNSMITH	#17: SILVER WAR	$2.50
☐ 30908-9	THE GUNSMITH	#18: HIGH NOON AT LANCASTER	$2.50
☐ 30909-7	THE GUNSMITH	#19: BANDIDO BLOOD	$2.50

Prices may be slightly higher in Canada.

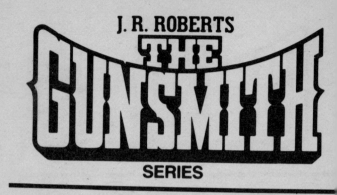

J. R. ROBERTS

THE GUNSMITH

SERIES

Prices may be slightly higher in Canada.